My
Many
Kisses

And Other Short Stories

By
Johnny Dolphin

s⃒ɒ

SYNERGETIC PRESS

Santa Fe, New Mexico

First edition.
Published by Synergetic Press
7 Silver Hills Road
Santa Fe, NM 87505 USA

www.synergeticpress.com

Cover design by Elemental Graphics.
Cover photo of Johnny Dolphin by Marie Harding.

ISBN 0 907791 29 8

Johnny Dolphin is the *nom de plume* of John Allen – poet, playwright, savant, inventor and co-founder of Biosphere 2, world's largest laboratory for global ecology. He has over two dozen publications to his credit, about half of them scientific, the rest in poetry, drama, prose, and film. His books are available through Synergetic Press–www.synergeticpress.com or your local bookstores.

Other Books by the Author

<u>Poetry</u>

> *Off the Road* (1989-2000)
> *Dream and Drink of Freedom*
> *Wild* (Poetry, Short Stories and Aphorisms)

<u>Fiction</u>

Trilogy of the '60s:
> *39 Blows on a Gone Trumpet*
> *Journey Around an Extraordinary Planet*
> *Liberated Space*

<u>Drama</u>

Caravan of Dreams Theater Plays
> Gilgamesh, Marouf the Cobbler, Faust Part One (V.1)
> Billy the Kid, Metal Woman, Tin Can Man (V.2)

<u>Non-Fiction (J.Allen)</u>

Space Biospheres, with Mark Nelson
Biosphere 2: The Human Experiment (Penguin Books)
Succeed: Handbook of Structuring Managerial Thought

Table of Contents

My Many Kisses

May, 1970

My Many Kisses is the story of a slightly disguised actual woman of today, about thirty, who analyzed and used her kisses in the way that Stendhal and Casanova analyzed and used their fucks. The protagonist first realized the power of kisses from the butterfly fluttering of her excited mother's lips which when she smiled and gooed in response resulted in increases of pleasurable lip stroking by her mother. She found the same to be true of her father and even more of her brother.

She became expert by the age of eight in rapturously accepting kisses and on occasion bestowing a random, thoughtful, or surprising kiss, and then quickly walking away to leave the recipient thinking about her in a manner she found thrilling to guess.

At ten in a church camp she found that the transfer of lipstick to a boy's lips and face by a certain pressure of her lips brought a rush of popularity. Sometimes the boy would not wash it all off and would gaze at her as if she were his sole object of contemplation for minutes on end.

Engrossed with deductions from these observations and experiments, and remaining equipped with a certain no-no that remained intact throughout high school, she experimented deeply with all forms of the kiss, both taken and given. She had found a path combining freedom with honor and safety. By combining kisses and dances, she became able to choose her consorts. She chose boys who did their science, excelled in adventures, or in theater. Her voice grew deep and thrilling. She chose a girl friend who adored and imitated her and whom she initiated into the power of her kisses. Her family remained certain of her freely expressed affection, her father and brother feeling faintly guilty enough to avoid interfering with her friends. Her mother compared her kisses with the cold pecks received by her friends from their daughters and refrained from undue nagging.

Naturally in college, she found ways to combine safely her expertise in kisses with occasional deeper experiments, but she never "threw herself away on a man" since however deep the new experiences, they were only somewhat, not infinitely, more satisfying. She continued to use her discretion, and found that oral transmission from scholars, champions, and artists was indeed the best way to comprehend knowledges, self-trainings, and forms of being. By her senior year, she found she was transmitting such teachings as well as receiving.

Obtaining a proposition to travel around the world for a year with a wealthy young connoisseur of art, she accepted with relish, and with a judicious yet spontaneous kiss here and there added as much to his circle of acquaintances as his wealth and degrees did to hers. After Asia and Europe, they separated in Swinging London, when one of her kisses resulted in the transfer of a tab of acid to her tongue, and she reached the point beyond giving and taking. She kissed a tree in St. James Park, the nose of a bronze lion in Trafalgar Square, and the foggy sky.

Meeting a man of parts, she traveled with him to Mexico, where two years later she kissed her baby. A year later she kissed the man goodbye, both swearing lifelong friendship, and she received a flat in London with two bedrooms, as well as kitchen, bath, and parlor. The kitchen and bath she tiled. She received fifteen thousand pounds a year to rear the child. She kissed him for that, never asked for a penny more, and immediately got a bicycle for a present and her choice of fifty books to start her own library. She kissed each book as she bought it at Skoobs, Blackwells, or Watkins.

As the story ends, she is on her fifth trip around the world. On the second she kissed the Blarney Stone, the third the Pope's ring, and on the fourth, the feet of a sage. She performs a tantric breathing exercise now when she kisses. She has wisely invested the few extra thousand pounds bestowed using the free advice of a stockbroker whom she kissed in gratitude. She has kissed over a hundred mushrooms, and more than two hundred peyote buttons. She throws two parties a year and kisses all her friends who come. She grows herbs and tomatoes in her window and kisses them daily. She kisses her special men and her special daughter in her special way, randomly, thoughtfully, surprisingly. She says when the time comes she will kiss her life goodbye.

A MAN WHO JUST SAID NO

June, 1984

This story follows the life of George Doodle. George, a tall black-haired man, graduated from Stanford in 1967 to become a computer analyst. By 1982 he's a millionaire and sits on foggy summer nights in his house in a redwood grove in the hills above Stanford.

George had never gotten drunk in his life, but in the early seventies he had started to buy himself an occasional recommended bottle of wine, which he sipped. George had always used a condom for his various nocturnal expeditions he undertook when he felt he might turn into a full-time masturbator. Nonetheless, between forays, he worked at developing a realistic masturbation and became quite adept at visualization although he was convinced that the two times he had experienced a materialization were only intense hallucinations and not tantric enlightenment.

George started thinking of getting a girl friend or of getting married. He had worked out the program in his mind. He did not want to become a homosexual and he had noticed his eyes spending more time on handsome lithesome young men. He could get a sound, reliable woman who would take care of him and probably want two kids. He could afford that. His nocturnal forays cost him a good percentage of income anyway. He had never believed in romance, except that of the magic of numbers manipulating measured portions of reality, so there would be nothing to miss that really existed outside his wishful thinking.

He had never taken acid, heroin, morphine, marijuana, cocaine, or smoked tobacco. He had sat in on the edge of all these kind of sessions, but had just said no. Some of his friends said some of these were "sacred" and that junk and its derivatives "profane," but some of his other friends took junk once in a while. He cracked a saturnine joke once to a colleague, that some of his friends had abused a drug, but no drug had abused them as far as he knew. He himself had taken speed once to see if he did mathematics better and quicker. It was a little quicker, but no better. Still an A+.

He had walked through Haight-Ashbury while it was being built, at its height, and during its dissolution. Its coming and going convinced him that everything, no matter how colorful, passed away so why invest emotion in what would be lost? He had always suspected this was the truth, but now he felt he had experimentally confirmed it.

He thought of suicide, studied the various methods, and found no logical reason against it, but he said no to that also.

He liked his five redwood trees. He liked silence. He had thought about joining the Sierra Club to save other people's redwoods but he didn't agree with all their actions.

He could have gotten rich at one point by switching companies to get a great stock option, but he thought lots of money stacked away was another trip not really real, not as good as acid from all reports, and he didn't see how he could figure any better way to distribute lots of money than whoever got it anyway. There were too many variables and so the economic system was too chaotic for anyone, even a top mathematician, to predict what set of results would occur from any given action.

Finally as the dawn begins to glimmer, George makes up his mind. First he will go the Unitarian Church and to the Stanford library until he sees the girl that he can talk to and who is looking for a decent, smart, not bad looking millionaire to marry and raise two children with. Only such a girl would have demonstrated that she possessed a truly compatible mathematical mind, whether or not she had formally developed it. He almost smiled to himself. He hadn't done badly in life by scientific evolutionary standards. He was not the best, but he was a good catch that could be calculated upon. She would not be the best, but she would be in the upper twenty percentile.

He paused for a last survey and critique of his thoughts and wishes. The unpredictable role of accidents could wreck everything. But probabilistically speaking, he had covered his bets. The odds weighed heavily in his favor. George stirred with satisfaction. It was 9 - 1, he calculated roughly, at last intuitively, that he would win the battle of life.

A Life Unknown by and Unknowable to the Intelligentsia

August, 1973

This tale is about Eddie, a half-Dutch half-Sioux American from the Dakotas. He had been in the last group of the U.S. Army's special unit trained just after World War II in all the methods of oriental schools of quick killing. Then the Army got scared of its products and shut down the school. He and the others had been given an identity card stating Professional Killer under their photo. He had to report to the sheriff of any county he stayed overnight in outside his home county.

After a fire in an aircraft carrier off Shanghai just before it fell, he had been declared dead at the age of twenty after burning in flames, but somehow had twitched before they threw him in the bag. He liked to say, "I know what it is to die and to live."

Eddie had a fourth grade education because his old man had run a wildcat drill rig and Eddie had been so bright and helpful that the old man would always raise a laugh from curious onlookers when he'd point to the kid working and say, "Couldn't find a better man. No, nor a cheaper one," he'd slyly add when the laughter died down. The mother had died. Eddie grew up wild and technical, savvy with pipes, trucks, drills, emergencies, accidents, weather, and Saturday night girls. On enlisting at eighteen, he immediately went to the top specialist training camps in the Army. His old man kept a small ranch, between drilling jobs, out in the Wyoming plains, so Eddie knew all about horses and cows, as well as a good deal about wheat.

Out of the Army, he faced down the old man, got ten thousand to start up with, bought a Ford pickup and a Marlin 30-30, married a blazing blonde he'd picked up at a saloon, and made a down payment on a hundred and sixty acre farm in Washington. Wheat.

Two good years, Marshall Plan for Europe supporting the price, rain at the right time, Eddie brilliant in all his farm strategies. Added another hundred and sixty acres. A new car. The wife slept with a neighbor and he caught her one afternoon. She wanted a divorce and half the property. He said, "Sure." That night she'd left and Eddie, after making all the property over to her name, burnt down the house, exploded the tractor and truck, burnt the barn, the wheat in the field, and hightailed it away. "That was my half I burnt," he said.

He landed in Las Vegas. His army outfit had been full of top gamblers, as cool and slit-eyed as they come. For a year his object was to make a thousand dollars a night and spend it all each night on a different blonde. Nearly every day he achieved his objective. He got tired of money and cunt.

Back with his father who had a sub-contract laying BIG INCH, the great gas line from Texas to Chicago, he became the real boss of the company in the field and learned to talk to lawyers, accountants, and tough contractors "who knew every trick in the book to pad their bills." He learned to think big and small at the same time. He learned that he was smarter than these guys in suits and ties who acted so tough and shrewd. And he knew he was tougher than they were. That they didn't stand a chance with him if it came to blows. They'd be dead quick. So Eddie never lost his temper no matter the shit he took. He said, "It's remarkable how good natured it makes you, knowing you can kill the other guy at any moment." He smiled friendly and kept up the talk and looked for openings. If he got cornered, he slid down on his seat around the table of suits, visualized killing each person in quick detail, then, relaxed in mind and body as he'd been taught, relived his dying in the aircraft carrier fire. At that point, something like white flames would blaze in his mind, and he would sit up and speak, integrating the situation, dominating the men there by his presence and thought. Then he strode out, smiling, on top and ready to make his next move. He stopped consulting the old man at all.

Eddie grew up in the oil business, but his imagination ran toward gold. Yellow gold excited him more than black gold. Lots of legends about lost gold mines floated around the bars in the West where tall booted men "passing through," stopped to talk with the right kind of "map", as they called a face.

One day a lawyer who had sized him up unrolled a map of a small mining district on the bar table in the back. He and Eddie talked about two hours. "Gold," the lawyer said. "Silver." "Lead and copper associated." This district had shut down in the great depression early in the century. Men starved and froze. One man bought it all up. Found murdered in 1917 at the bottom of a working shaft. The lawyer and his friends had bought it "for a song" five years ago. All they needed was the right man to run it. The lawyer was sure a fortune lay there soon because the price of gold would be turned over to the market by the U.S. government and the price would rise from thirty-five dollars to at least three hundred dollars an ounce. " We bought it just in time. The right man could get half, and we'd stake him for a three year start-up."

Eddie told him to bring all his maps and data for him to study.

That night Eddie had a dream. He discovered that he was on his seventeenth recurrent reincarnation to solve the problem of world poverty. The cause, his dream showed him, was the lack of gold, the consequent printing of paper money and letting inflation steal the savings of working people. The lack of gold was due to the cartel shutting down and closing mining districts by means sometimes such as murdering mine owners, but mainly it was due to their concealing techniques for extracting gold from finely disseminated deposits, where the gold was in tiny microscopic particles. Eddie dreamed he would discover for himself that method, that he would open up great gold open pits as had happened with copper on low grade deposits. He thus would eliminate that grand invisible thief of the people's work, inflation. The reason that it was his seventeenth reincarnation into exactly that time, place, and mission was revealed to him. He had failed sixteen times before, assassinated each time just as he had put it all together.

In China just after World War II he had saved the life of a Frenchman in Shanghai by quickly taking out two thugs attacking him in an alley. Eddie was on offshore leave from his ship. This man, Maurice, ran Interpol operations in Shanghai. He had given Eddie an Interpol card that Eddie would occasionally flash at U.S. police officers when he wanted special information.

Now he called Maurice who was excited by Eddie's move into gold. Maurice said, "We are after big frauds not only in gold but platinum. I will promote you, give you a better card, and you can track down these people and learn all you need to know about your mine at the same time."

Eddie had all the skills from his ranching and oil work needed to run a mine and mill except one. He could repair any kind of equipment, stay alert to danger from every direction, lift and lever weights, use explosives, crush, screen, grind, table, but he was new to fire and acids, the actual extraction of the precious metals. He had to learn sampling, fire assay, and how to handle dangerous acids and fumes.

He took samples he collected from the ore veins in the mine to the most famous and the most notorious assayers from Texas to California to Montana, using Maurice's secret list. He found the great texts on pyrometallurgy and assaying written before

1910, when they were written how to do it rather than as theory for engineers who would mechanize and automate the procedures both for efficiency and to hide what was being done in the interests of their employers: states, corporations, and "the octopus" – the cartel. Price and profits would be maximized by releases from stocks and rates of production whose manipulation was known only to the few in power or trusted by power.

Eddie turned over to Maurice the assay results that ranged from a tenth of an ounce of gold and platinum per ton (worthless) to those stating that 200 ounces per ton lay in his mine (fortune exceeding the caliphs). By Maurice's intervention and by Eddie's providing two beautiful ladies from his BIG INCH days to a powerful White House donor, he soon had one of the rarer government licenses, the right to touch fire to gold, in other words to amalgamate small flecks of gold into bricks, otherwise a highly illegal act. It was signed by the President and the Secretary of Treasury, Connally, who had just released gold on to the free market and whose price had indeed shot up.

The platinum also interested Eddie more and more because he found in the records of the mine that old shipments were sent all the way to San Francisco and thence transshipped to Wales which had one of the few platinum refineries in the 1880-1910 period. His interest became intense when he discovered the U.S. Geological Service identified platinum as a component of the ore in its 1900 book on the site, and had eliminated it in their 1940 edition.

Platinum brought the same price as gold, but in addition, was usually associated with an entire group of similar metals: palladium, osmium, iridium, rhodium, and rhenium. Osmium was deadly poisonous as a gas and it easily gasified. The very name of rhodium showed it had been discovered by the cartel. The uses of this group ranged from cracking oil catalytically to making the most superb pen points and jewelry. Eddie found the cartel consisted of organizations in four countries: the Soviet Union, U.S.A., South

Africa, and Columbia, with free access to London as its financial center.

In five years, Eddie had used up all the capital of the Illinois lawyer's group, which had only a few small pieces of gold to show for their efforts, but the mine had been almost single-handedly restored to working order. A laboratory with full crushing, grinding, concentrating, leaching, and assay capabilities stood in an ancient well-timbered building on site. The old mill had been restored enough that he could run a couple of tons a day through its furnaces. All with only the assistance of his two Apache ex-commandos, who doubled as night guards and a lady he had married for her business skills. The lady already had children. Eddie never played around any more. He devoted himself. He began to show the best of his assay results to big time investors.

Eddie invited them to the mine and set up a forty-eight hour continuous process where he single-handedly made small gold nuggets out of a five-ton pile of ore. He would get so concentrated he would eat only one sandwich in a day. It was roast beef. The potential investors, invited by twos or threes, would come out to watch. "Look!" Eddie would cry out, "I never lied to you yet. You check out my every move. You'll see the gold come out. All I need is ten million and we'll make billions. This whole range of little hills will become one big open pit. There'll be enough gold and platinum in the world to back every currency."

But none of the investors could stay awake for forty-eight hours. They would all fall asleep sooner or later and then they would wonder who could know exactly what Eddie had done? Maybe he had salted the gold in by hand. But why would he have risked so much by giving them full access if he was faking? Paranoia met with greed in crosswaves wrinkling their well-fed faces. But they would all finally pay up ten thousand or twenty thousand and keep it going. Eddie always was able to extract that much because at the end when he was down to getting the gold out of the last few pounds of concentrate, they would slowly rise as if by invisible command to stand there quietly, faces glistening with sweat, wide awake, mouths open, in full possession by gold fever, watching Eddie's every graceful move with acids, fire, and metal. Some would actually shake as if they had malaria. "Give me a man compounded of curiosity, ambition, loyalty, and greed," Eddie would say, "and I can do with him what I will."

Finally, four years later, Eddie flew to Denver to talk directly with the president of one of the great corporations in the mining industry. His briefcase carried several one-ounce samples, one sample each of gold, platinum, palladium, rhodium, rhenium, osmium, and iridium. At even a half-ounce per ton, billions of dollars worth of it ran throughout the entire intrusive zone.

Three big boys in suits hired a small plane on the spot to fly with Eddie to the mine. That night Eddie died with a bullet hole in the forehead. The local paper announced that a Mr. Miller had suddenly passed away in bed in the arms of his Savior. No investigation was made into his death. The samples disappeared and the mine shut down again as it had in 1917.

A broad-shouldered man sat in the back at the funeral flanked by two other broad-shouldered men. He was the man who had financed Eddie for six months two years before. Well-connected in Washington, his private police force was rated one of the best and guarded an entire city he had built for "snowbirds" in Nevada.

All of the buildings, including the lavishly constructed one of 1885, that allowed entry to the mine, disappeared soon after Eddie's death. Only a two hundred foot deep hole in the ground remained in view, surrounded by thousands of tons of yellow-brown gangue from the old days, sixty to eighty years before.

The Man Who Loved Emotions

December, 1969

Gerard Manley believed that all of the argued about ideas that passed for judgment, knowledge, and wisdom were wrong. This thought had flashed on him at the age of fifteen while he scrounged thick paper-shelled pecans off the chill October brown grass beneath the grove of straight-trunked pecans that stood by themselves on the small ten acre flat on Rush Creek, so named because of the rushing waters after a cloudburst which also usually flooded the flat so that no home was built there.

Over the years he'd worked here and there throughout the western states, plains, mountains, and deserts, reading voraciously his paperback classics jammed in his blue jean jacket pockets and passing many a Saturday afternoon in a local library. Gerard had developed four or five buddies and two or three steady girls, depending on how you counted steady, over that decade of wandering and observation of himself in his many moods, nature in its various spectacularities, and girls and guys in a number of dramatic manifestations.

He hadn't written much, actually only some scraps, but he always thought he'd wind up writing, for whom, he never quite figured out. The next generation sounded real good to him for his audience. The generation he had been biologically assigned to was clearly going to blow it in the clutch historically. He could see his contemporaries had no staying power as he worked around from 1955-65, logging, fire fighting, dam building, repairing heavy equipment, watching lonely stretches of national forests, running into all kinds of them here and there. When their moment came to enter history, they'd crack under pressure. The next generation who came in would want to know the intimate details of why and how they'd goofed it. He would be able to write about it because he'd seen how they had gotten it all wrong, and from that traced back how all the humans since they'd left the tribal magic had gotten it all wrong even though they'd gotten certain parts very right.

Now that America was pulsing the beat of earth's destiny, all that wrongness was honing in on it. On the other hand, thanks to the fascists, communists, and generals in white Mercedes chasing all their best thinkers and artists to the Home of the Free and the Land of the Brave, America was being given the best the world had to offer, and learning fast. He had to laugh. American abstract artists got their rocks off reducing the European cube to the plane, the plane to a line and the line to color, eliminating the total content of western civilization.

He wasn't against any of that. But he thought all of it was too American, too provincial, to make sense to a planetary world. A super in-joke to play on New York. He heard Ginsberg intone about how he and "Jack Kerouac sat in a garbage dump and looked at a rusty tin can" and then Kerouac set out in a car to a Mexican whorehouse, after that speeding through lonely America from San Francisco to New York stopping only in Denver and New Orleans. He preferred Mark Twain and Pudd'n Head Wilson. He preferred Jack London and the Sea Wolf. He preferred Rimbaud and Abyssinia, Miller and Paris and Burroughs and Interzone Tangier to the City Lights Bookstore and North Beach. He preferred Coleman to Charlie Parker.

In 1965, he turned thirty, the year you had to become a poet or quit. He drank a bottle of Port, heavy, sweet, slowly for hours before he fell, plastered, on the sand in an arroyo on a clear starry night.

Yesh, he muttered to himself, why all the ideas are wrong is nobody ever had a real idea about emotions. Yesh, everyone was emotional, suppressing or suffusing emotions, but nobody saw that emotions are an entire independent world of world views. Each emotion is a world view. Each emotion is a separate real look into a separate reality!

Yesh, each emotion is a drug specialist that supplies a certain matrix of hormones, of messages, of information, that sets a different beat to the heart, drenches the brain with molecules that activate and deactivate different sets of synapses, shifts shapes perceived, stretches or quickens time noted, finds a different science in each number, a new thrill or threat in ever y gesture.

He wrote his poem that night. He realized the Seven Deadly Sins were Seven Worlds of emotion, and that each emotional set, the vanities, greeds, lusts, angers, prides, sloths, and gluttonies, contained two pathways of seven major beats each, one leading to all systems on go and one to complete shutdown of all systems except for the aimless squirting of the remaining hormones that careened through a shipwrecked human.

Gerard fell in love with his vision, his discovery of the universes of emotion. He wrote and rewrote his poem of ninety-eight words, seven times seven times two. Each word had to equal any of the others in power to excite the emotion's full chemical charge. He lay in the arroyo till the hot noon sun chased him out, unshaven, hungry, and sweating. He walked back five miles over the desert to Cottonwood and its diner with its fried eggs, ham, biscuits, gravy, bottomless cup of coffee, and orange juice served by its strong-boned waitress, wrinkling-eyed with pert satirical glances.

"Me," he whispered, ecstatic. That word, Me, had started his chain reaction discovery of the power of loving his emotions. It was the first word of his new poem. He had decided to read it out to the whatever part of the universe surrounded him at the rate of one word per day. "Me, me, me." Me was not an idea, he realized,

16

nobody could think about me, me was not a percept, nobody could see or hear me, me was not a movement. He moved an arm, a finger, a leg, a toe, an eyebrow, undulating his whole body, nowhere could he move me. But when he said "Me," his entire emotional world changed. By continuously saying "me, me, me," silently so no one would know what he was doing, not even Miss Sharpeyes, and by saying "me," in fact he now saw that she was not "the waitress," but Miss Sharpeyes, giving him the once, twice, and thrice-over, once for his unironed jeans and unshaved skin, twice to gauge his sex potential, and thrice as a potential troublemaker and low tipper. The diner was no longer a "greasy spoon" in nowheresville, it was wonderfully designed for me to study me in the mirror, for me to look out the broad window for possible rides to take me the first stage to wherever me wanted. The crossroads outside showed me a paved way back east, out west, and an adventurous gravel way down south and up north, and me sat at the center where all these routes would return to if me took one of them and kept right on going in spite of hell, high water, sandstorms, or blizzards all the way around the planet.

"Me" literally allowed me to be at the center of the universe because if me looked above me kept going to one edge of everything and if me looked below me kept going to the opposite edge. He realized "me" was that magic carpet that he'd read about, fascinated, and talked about on occasion with his friend David when they walked in the golden dusk-filled gloaming on the low levee by the side of Rush Creek and dreamed of how they at least would escape to far away and far out places and adventures and girls and ideas. But they had never seen what material that magic carpets could be woven from. David had dwindled proudly and he had roamed in vanity.

Now he knew. Me included everything it wished to. Ginsberg's Howl could be part of me as much as Brion Gysin's Process, as much as Basho's lonely Zen sneaking up on frogs for company, as much as Dostoyevsky's passionate groups hacking God and History. Me bowed to Miss Sharpeyes, made a motion of shaving, and said how about it if I stay overnight here in town and she smiled yes to me, and he knew that before she'd have said no to him, strong as he was and smart as he was, and that his poem had already begun to work miracles on him such as he had always known real poetry could do for poets and that was why poets kept arising and to him real poets were higher than prophets because where was the prophet who had benefited from his prophecy?

At the end of ninety-seven days he had come to the last word in his poem. A novel could describe each day but this story will end with the last day. Gerard had been carried by his magic carpet to Quebec, Paris, Carnac, London, New York, Mexico City, the Windriver Mountains, the Crow reservation, the Bitterroots, the Snake River Wilderness, a secret enclave in Sonoma, and now he was cruising in the early morning with a newfound friend over the Golden Gate Bridge into San Francisco where the word was, It's Here that it's gonna happen, Now, in 1967.

"Drop me off at Golden Gate Park," he said.

The last word in his poem was appetite. "Appetite, appetite, appetite," he said over and over till it became silent and then he engraved it on his heart so he could read it visually as well as hear it.

Since the magic carpet, if truly magic, would fly him everywhere, at the end, if appetite failed he might just as well, no better, have "stood in bed." He understood why the French always said "bon appetite," that was what made their life poetry so that it had become the second home to all who wished to learn to live. He came across a group of ten wonderfully dressed, each different, people sitting in one of the secluded open areas. Appetite, appetite, he had an appetite for that rare flavor that emanated from them and from each one of them. He stopped and let them one and all come into him. Appetite, appetite.

He slowly sat down at their edge in his blue jeans and boots, with his blanket roll. None of them smiled and none of them frowned and none of them talked and none of them stared. He felt an appetite for me. He needed more me to fly his magic carpet from the edge to within this group of living, breathing, sensing, thinking and, yes, he felt for a certainty, emotion grokking beings. What else could a poet's appetite find so beckoning?

He sat with them for a long while. Appetite, appetite. Two of the longhaired women opened up the hampers at their side; one began to pour some wine into cups and the other to slice some cheese and bread. He began to rise but first he murmured appetite, appetite, appetite. He caught the eye of first one and then another around the irregular circle. The lady with the wine pointed that there were only ten cups. The man at his side offered him to share his cup.

He slowly drank his sip. They all smiled. Appetite, appetite. His was whetted to Samurai sharpness. His magic carpet had landed him in life's banquet. His poetry had found its people.

The Man Who Always Failed

April, 1983

Jeff Stengel always failed but that never stopped him from starting up new projects. For one thing, all his projects nearly worked. They failed only in sight of succeeding. Jeff's considered opinion was that they failed because he was always twenty or more years "ahead of his time." On the other hand he said, "Failure never hurts me because it happened twenty years 'before my time' and so failure stays always behind me, just like succeeding stays twenty years ahead of me, and so I stay free."

Some friends of his stayed on with his projects that failed because they believed in twenty years their time would come, and the projects had all accumulated productive assets. The problem was that no cash flow above maintenance costs seemed to come. This low cash flow involved a life style of minimum expenditures and lots of hands-on care. Other friends departed after five or ten years getting by on their wits by either selling off assets or running them in a very different way they thought would bring in the cash flow.

Jeff's secret for finding his special kind of projects was that he looked for an alignment between what he needed for his thinking and poetry to make the next step in their development and what "knot" some culture and ecoregion and technosystem needed to untie to make the next step in their historical development. Jeff was convinced that "taking the long haul view and taking the whole earth into consideration" showed that humanity did have a definite and positive historical development. He also became convinced that there was a lot more creative history that could be made if certain "knots" could be untied before they choked a potentiality to death.

Jeff called this approach Supply Side economics rather than Demand side. This was why all the projects failed to turn a profit. What Jeff supplied may have been needed, and there were always a few intelligent people who could raise some capital and would work at it who thought so, but the public couldn't demand it without knowing why and what it was, and how come it was worth the price. Since the projects were always new, there was a built-in time lag in the best possible case. In the worst possible case, there was no market demand possible for several decades. "If ever" some of his friends ironically added.

Jeff started up the Tepee and Nomad Theater Troupe with a hot San Francisco dancer and an Action Artist lady from the Village on a small farm they managed to put a down payment on in the Poconos. The Tepee was a hundred feet in diameter supported by aluminum poles. Its fabric was waterproofed and fire-resistant and its hardwood floors were sprung so that dancers would not damage their feet and ankles. The stage could be the whole flat space with spectators interspersed, or a colored light extravaganza scene focused on the players with moveable bleachers. They got about fifteen actors together and they built well-insulated houses a la Frank Lloyd Wright together with an organic garden and chickens "to cut start-up costs." The bus became a super job, blue and red with a fighter pilot's cockpit roof put in the center so someone could sit up there and watch the scenery if they wished. Jeff's big idea was "continuous creativity."

If they became world famous, everyone would want to come to the Tepee and they could have standing room only for three months, twice a day. Then they could tour for three months. Three months off for traveling to find "new material" and then three months setting up the year's three new productions.

In the late sixties and early seventies they made out. Doing all their own stage, electric, mechanical, costume, garden, cooking, and housework their costs were as low as they could be. The initial capital to buy the place and get the materials and tools he got by giving 50% of the ownership to the investor.

Then the universities shut down their campuses to "unofficial" touring theaters. The Tepee's policy of continually changing their plays meant their hits never paid big, and the not-hits got as much play as the hits. The Tepee was found exciting, even legendary, only in certain circles, certain small circles.

The Tepee became finally a well-known restaurant, the houses a small artists' colony for writers, and the bus just wore out. Some of the actors moved to New York or Los Angeles, the others got married and went to work. Jeff stayed good friends with the dancer and artist who kept the artists' colony when the Investor called it quits and took the Tepee as his recompense. Jeff got an annual dinner at the Tepee and two weeks stay a year at the colony out of it plus five years of adventures and insights. He was happy about it all.

Then he got into energy with a couple of guys and designed windmills and solar devices to generate electricity. For a hundred grand he got an obscure patch of windswept dirt out in West Texas with a three bedroom frame house that needed a lightning rod and for another hundred grand, an old windmill (five thousand), an old milling machine, lathe, grinder, workbench and tools (ten thousand), a pickup (five thousand), a stove, three beds, and a library (five thousand), which left them seventy-five thou for three years operating capital. He put a couple of weaned calves out to forage to raise some beef for the next year. They shot a deer apiece each year for venison.

In six months they were running off their energy system. In a year, it looked pretty good. Some government funds came their way from the big scare over oil in seventy-three. What Jeff was inventing was an eco-energy system for a ranch, or a village, an area with the right amount of wind and sun, to support itself. Jeff never tried to invent merely a technical improvement the existing market could snap up. He thought the existing market was the problem, that advertising driven demand and the Fed increasing cash produced a cancerous expansion of things that ate up people. He wanted people, so to speak, to eat up the things necessary for a cultured existence.

Everybody who came out to visit Solar Wind liked the experience, but couldn't figure out why this was better than pushing a button, or if they could figure that out they didn't need any consulting since they could do it themselves, because they'd already seen how Jeff did it.

Jeff and his two buddies wound up making over the entire solar and wind power patch to the investor for twenty grand for get away money plus their personal hand tools and the library. The house had all been fixed up, its energy costs were low, Jeff had re-grassed the land and planted some fruit trees ("the best solar energy collector," he called them) that he watered from solar energy pump irrigation. The investor sold the property for four hundred thousand a year later. He told Jeff this time he was fifty years ahead of his time. The price of oil was going down again and it'd take a real collapse of fossil fuel reserves to make the price high enough to make energy developments pay based on local wind and sun power.

With what Jeff learned from his continuous creativity theater and his continuous discontinuous energy production unit, he decided to put them both together, add earthquake proofing and waste recycle and build a non-tourist tourist hotel in a colorful area of Asia that few people yet came to. The market might have liked to travel but that was costly in time and money so what the market would pay for was tourism which everybody hated because it destroyed as usual with these type of products everything that it touched, but, of course, it did generate beaucoup cash and got people away from European offices and factories where they contemplated useless repetitions of their supervisors and bosses. Even tourism would be better than that deadly routine and so tourism spread for the same reasons that white bread did, namely making really good bread took too much time, but lots of bread was needed.

Jeff's idea was to invent a hotel so interesting that it would be not just sleeping rooms but the destination itself so that the tourist would become an inhabitant of the area and so economical that many local people would come by. These tourists would be accepted because they would be living in a place local people also liked to come to talk, eat, groove, grok, make out, make dates, read, entertain, see or be part of theater, go to meetings or sessions by local artists or scientists. Living in the hotel would be like living in a hot spot of the culture that they'd come to see, a real encounter place, where who knew whom would turn up next. Of course, it wouldn't be the past, but it would be something new that grew out of that past and included impacts from other cultures, which the old culture itself now wanted and needed.

He managed to get a half million of the capital for 50%, the land from members of a local tribe for 25% and his promise he would show them how to quality control their handicraft business, and 25% for his friends he would need to design and set up the EastWest Hotel. He drilled a thousand foot well to avoid diarrhea complaints, added an ozonated filter for good measure, recycled the waste from his squat toilets (economical and healthy), made ten rooms without a shower for super-low prices to attract long-term intelligentsia, set up a sauna he personally carried in for the delectation of the hill hikers who would come in from the far back country, and collected a library of the main mystics of the three local religions plus western literature from Gilgamesh to Burroughs and Smith and Marx to Schumpeter and Hayek, Heraclitus and Macchiavelli to Jefferson and Spengler.

He and his team lived in two tribal thatched huts while they built the hotel and watched the magicians watch them and breathed a sign of relief when the magicians okayed it. They knew they were okayed when the top magician asked if he could run the library. A bigger sign came when the artisans decided they did want the hotel built the right way and started to show them exactly what could be done with scrap marble and old wood and stopped taking off every week on the excuse of religious holidays. An old painter of the dancing and wrathful deities agreed to paint the restaurant as he would have done a temple. Finally, a dancer agreed to teach his lore in the Long House Theater.

After a year's startup EastWest became a word-of-mouth place. In the next five years EastWest became a living legend. "In" from Berlin to Kyoto to East Village. "In" with anyone who wished to be with it from the ten local cultures. Occasionally a great teacher or shaman would appear for a week with his students. The down river singers with hashish stoked religious ecstasy came up once a year to the packed, hushed courtyard.

The investor finally kicked them out. The market had discovered EastWest. The local national laws had been re-written. Only invested capital now counted in ownership. Suddenly the investor owned eighty percent and had total control. The toilets were changed to Western "thrones," and a new clientele with gold credit cards arrived. The sauna became a room. The accountant found no profit in the hikers. The ten rooms for long-term intelligentsia became five apartment rooms bringing in four times as much. The new clientele did not like surprises.

Jeff had failed again. His tribal friends waved him goodbye from their feast made specially for him. They still owned ten percent. Suddenly Jeff realized that he was not only the man who always failed. From another angle he had always won. He wished he could interest others in winning the way that he had won. He had never regretted a project. He had always learned a lot, made lifelong friends and felt useful. But he couldn't help wondering why he, and his friends who bet on him, couldn't really win, win all the way. He decided that's what he would learn to do, but even if he failed at that, still with whatever flowed anew from the fire he would go on the next project. Connected, somehow, to infinity, he never felt cornered. Finish one thing, and on to the next was his surefire way out. It was even the best chance to work with death.

A Girl Who Said Yes

May, 1973

Of course, Sharon Field did not always say yes, but she did say two very big yesses by the time she was twenty. She said those yesses in a way that all of her was saying yes, and she kept on saying that yes if she felt like it even when surrounded by no. She got by with it because she treated these special yesses like a military campaign. She kept track of her conquests and casualties, and changed her strategies to achieve her objectives according to the result's feedback. And she understood new wars are lost by using the last war's weapons.

The Koran distinguishes two holy wars, the lesser one an external war against aggressors and the greater one an internal war of the deeper against the shallower, the truer against the less true. Sharon fought both kinds of war at once. She fought her wars inside herself with the aim of becoming more of what she could be. Naturally sometimes this involved the lesser war having to deal with most difficult problems.

Her first big yes came under a peach tree in brilliant bloom on a sunny still chilly day against the shale cliffs rising four thousand feet into the blue sky, turtle-backed against rain and wind by its capping strata of a sheer three hundred feet face of quartzific sandstone. A geologist once read those cliffs to her like a book, an ancient book with incredible fairy tale stories of giant reptiles and billions of tons of oil locked in the shale and two hundred million years of time creating these architectures of space.

She said yes to life when she was twelve. She had touched some blood on her thigh and knew what it was. She looked at the pink blossoms and saw blood and blossoms sharing a blue sky that drew her into a shape-shifting vortex.

A tomboy never out of her bluejeans once she pulled them on in the morning, she knew that now she'd have to start learning how to be a girl. Everybody had told her she'd have to straighten up and fly right. She had used her eyes. She hadn't stood around with her thumb up her rump. She'd have to allow herself to be looked at instead of looking, of mastering a dreamy gaze when a boy stared into her eyes, of following on the dance floor, of mastering a dialogue with the mirror about her face for whatever event, about her hair, about her dress. She would have to learn to figure out what boys wanted, how much she would let them get, how to date and have fun while keeping up her studies, her reading, her lonely hikes into the high desert where she slipped her body into the world the same way she slipped her hand into a glove, and she and the world worked together the way her hand and glove did in the garden where she worked every Saturday morning with her mother pruning, trimming, potting, composting, pausing to contemplate shapes, spaces, colors, vitality and disease, the different species and the fountain and the big sandstone rocks her father had brought in with a truck that had a crane on the back.

In this memory warp and future woof she had textiled herself a mandala rug like she'd seen on the floor of the anthropologist who had spent three months in the Junction. When he'd invited her to stare at the rug she had been furtively glancing at, she'd entered a strange space in the center of her head which was so dancing with change and strange that she became amazed at its vivid clarity as if there were a point in the midst of all that swirl that kept all dizziness at bay and effortlessly created a phantasmagoria of delights that somehow were so real that her body glowed with their energy. The blood on her finger was the still point in thousands of pink blossoms glittering gently against, almost in, the large large blue and her Yes was to that point, to her sexual body, to her human body, to her memories and to her futures. She stretched her forefinger as high as it would stretch into the sky and felt herself begin to rotate. She would become a magic stroboscope attenuating a flashing yellow sun with the deep blue above the tawny cliff. She spun until she stopped, rigid with ecstasy, stepped outside herself and for a brief endless moment saw everything. How she loved the young girl who stood there so lithely in the afternoon hush, in a silence so deep she could hear the silence.

Somehow as easily as if following a web laid down by an all-knowing spider her days strolled into a felicitous pattern exemplifying an America of Song of Myself that had not even a suspicion of a mad Ahab chasing a white whale throughout the abysmal waters of the world ocean.

She had become Queen of the Homecoming Game, been belle of the ball that night, and kissed the captain of the team passionately exhaustlessly as Begin the Beguine played over and over on the record player in the living room.

Sharon then went to a beautiful college in the mountains for the sons and daughters of the solidly well-off, and in time became the most popular girl in her sorority.

Her junior year, because she had learned French the best in her class, she won a prize to go to Paris for a semester. There she read Rimbaud. "We are the race that never became Christians. We sang under torture." She could not understand how those few words seized her as nothing had since she touched her first sexual blood. She touched her blood again but with a different finger, an invisible finger, but a finger that she could see even better. A finger drenched in a colorless blood that sang like the wind in the pines on the Continental Divide. A finger that stretched up into a black sky pierced by a million stars, a sky that boded revenge for crimes she could not imagine and raptures for joys she could not remember.

29

Where her heart had been she felt empty space and in that small empty exultation she felt huge enough to enter the world, the entire world. She wandered out into the Rive Gauche making herself available to that revenge and rapture.

Revenge meant reconquer. Where had she been conquered that she must reconquer? Where had she been ruptured that now she must enrapture?

A lean dark-haired student in his sweater and army jacket startled up from leaning against a urine-stained wall on the Rue de Bonaparte and began stalking her as she glided in some weightless way impelled by repeating "Sang under Torture," "Sang under Torture." The Christians had tortured some "race", but this "race" still sang. What kind of people would Christians torture and how then could they still sing? She had toured the dungeons with their torture instruments in Paris. Who had overcome these torturers and taken out those instruments into the light and burnt those monasteries of the Inquisition? America suddenly seemed a vanilla ice-cream stand in a dark half-finished surrealist painting, the sunny half was missing. Of course, Kennedy had just been shot.

She turned right at the river and her stalker was now matching her stride for stride ten feet behind her. She knew that for her this was Rimbaud reincarnate. She felt the invisible finger inside her beckoning him to follow. Since he clearly could see that as well as she, he must also see that black sky, feel revenge and rapture. She varied her rhythm like a master choreographer for a block and he never missed a beat. Sure of his stalking her invisibly as well as visibly she turned solely to the thoughts that had taken command of her body.

Why could she know so well the meaning of revenge? She had never been conquered. She was American. That meant and she nearly fell to the pavement from her realization that she had been conquered the moment she was born. She had been born into a conquered nation. That nation had outwardly conquered a continent of Indians and enslaved half a continent of blacks, but innerly they had been conquered by a shamanic craft and a Yoruban possession music. At her elite social college they had laughed going to visit a ceremony of the Northern Cheyenne and going to nightclubs to hear Charles Mingus and John Coltrane. The leather-skinned cowboys had grinned in a certain way when she and her sorority friends went riding at a ranch surviving only by taking a few dudes on a ride now and then.

She had flown on like an owl in the evening loosed upon the meadow mice but her stalker now loosely danced along beside her. Never looking at him as he drew ever closer her emanations outdid his radiations so much that finally he with a sigh let out an actual piece of himself, unaltered by pride or vanity.

At the Pantheon she stopped to gaze down upon the buildings where not only Rimbaud but Baudelaire and Villon had also both searched and fled throughout the night. At twenty she was two years older than Rimbaud when he stabbed out those lines. She felt ancient as all hell. What had she done with her life? What had they done with her life? She had been tortured and not only by Christians, but she had not sung, she had swayed along with records like a fish in a school of fish.

He faced her six inches away. She stared back into his eyes and sailed forward into an empty space protected by menacing guardians, his ferocious allies, grimacing, on the alert along the edges.

"I belong to the race that was never Christian", she said in English.

"Oui," he said.

"We sang under torture."

He began to sing, "Moi, en la coeur d'une étrangère..."

"Oui," she said. "Yes."

This second yes gave her two people, the first yes the beautiful girl with her triumphant sexual blood discovering her

31

unity with sunny nature, and the second yes a wild seductive woman discovering her unity with poets of the city nights.

Jean Françoise not only introduced her to love but to cooking, to cuisine, to tasting and sipping, dalliance and perfume and flowers. And all with the satire and irony of revenge and the nostalgia for raptures forgone that rivaled raptures being undergone. He never asked her to marry him, he never discussed her family, he wanted her engagé for the time she had left in Paris.

"We have only this brief existence," he said, "so we must make sure we exist not drift into vagueness." He never intimated they would meet again. She could not believe her luck. Now she knew what "singing under torture" meant. She wrote fondly her précis of Rimbaud for Jean Françoise:

We humans have never believed the lies of any exploiters.

We live, real artists, for whatever time we can escape their police, their jails, their money, their propaganda.

He shook her hand without an embrace. She looked at him and he at her and they knew each other then turned decisively from each other to live in a different way their now forever altered destinies.

"I live and I exist," she sang to herself.

The Right Here and Now Mystic

October, 1977

Jack Branford thought Richard the Lionheart was the finest p oet:

> No prisoner can tell his honest thought
> Unless he speaks as one who suffers wrong;
> But for his comfort he makes a song.
> My friends are many but their gifts are nought.

And that Caesar was the exemplar as a prose stylist:

> All Gaul is divided in to three parts.
> I came, I saw, I conquered.

So he saw no reason to get out of the mining business where he was a powerful millionaire when he decided to become a mystic. After all since he did well in life then if he reached the point of genuine insight into and even union with the processes of reality that mystics were reputed to reach, even become a part of reality, he wouldn't have to describe his experiences in a stilted denominationally dogmatic language to keep his room, his position, his food and clothing coming, working for some organized hierarchy of power. He wouldn't have to cover his tracks and depend on a wink to tell people when he was telling the truth, and when he was having to mouth bullshit to save his ass. He was certain that if mysticism was for real, mystics saw and became the same kind of thing with individual and temperamental shades of difference in their manifestations just like all people who engaged in gold mining did the same things with their sampling, assays, acids, bases, and crucibles though some might be pokefaced while others grinned.

But still gold always came out as gold, not as sometimes silver, sometimes platinum, not on one occasion the Absolute, another the Immanent and on others the Unknowable. Those were big differences and the differences always happened to be something that could fit in with what the local ruling class insisted was "the truth" or else, like Al-Hallaj, the mystic who blew the hypocritical cover, they were butchered as a public example to encourage silence or else conformity in expression.

Jack used the same methods he had used so successfully to find, develop, and keep his gold and silver mine. He searched the big picture literature of the Sufis, the Tibetans, the Hindus, the Benedictines, and poets like Whitman, Blake, Rumi, and Li Po. Then he searched the technological literature, Nagarjung, Patanjali, the Exercises, the Book of the Dead. Then he hired a good geologist to personally show him the country. He made a donation of ten thousand dollars to the best Tibetan Rimpoche he found and took instructions. He trekked to a certain place in the Himalayas then took a train to another specialist in Mysore and studied Raja and Laya yogas and made appropriate presents which tested his discrimination and learned exact techniques of observing changes of state and centers and what exactly marked the transitions to the states and centers. He sat in Zen sessions in Kyoto. He stayed for a week with Benedictines in France. He bought enough rugs and got into their symbolism enough so that his rug dealer took him into the tekkia of his sheik where he learned about self-deceit and self-fraud so subtle and so complete it made the gold industry look like an ethical paradise. "This alone has been worth it," he said to himself, "to learn all of old Jack's tricks and games and how to spot new ones he invents. This alone will save me a fortune, not to speak of doubling my time to see what's real."

Then, since he had proved justified in his conclusion that temples and retreats were operated just as he operated his gold mine, that is for profit and the power to lead as free a life as possible in societies whiplashed by the Church, the State, and Family Oligarchies, he became strengthened in his resolve to stay in his mining enterprise while pursuing the mystic path. The great Sufis, even, had stated there were two ways, the safer way, the group, and the wilder way of Uwais, the individual recognized even by Mohammed who never met him, as solitary adept. Jack figured that if he had survived the gold industry, he really didn't need a group of melancholy ectomorphs to make things safer for himself. I like not yon Cassius, anyway, with his lean and hungry look, he smiled to himself.

The other sticking point to Jack was that he couldn't buy into an Absolute God (out of the solution) or an Immanent God (in each part of the solution) or an Everywhere God (Nothing but God) or into Nothingness or into any one all-embracing code word claiming to be The Truth. He couldn't bow down to that stuff.

He was going to bet on Reality. Whatever reality was, that's what he wished to be totally part of. And he wasn't going to make any prejudgments about that. He knew that he didn't know, feel, or see anywhere near reality. He had studied his science; he was a top structural and historical geologist. He had been married five years to a wonderful actress who had initiated him into all the arts including those of love, and he still saw her on occasion in Beverly Hills where, happily married to a great director, she introduced him from time to time to a new up and coming actress. He had studied his Cohen and Nagel on the limitations and power of logic, and how the experimental method of science was needed to establish the facts for genuine philosophy to incorporate in its efforts to think steadily and whole about the universe. But Jack realized he was in a body and that body was of incalculable importance and that neither art nor science nor philosophy knew anything of that body, how to deal with its death, and what was the relation of I to the Body and the Body to I. Jack was determined not to die without finding that out. The Body, by which he meant everything about it, its bones to the marrow, its flesh to the gene, its blood to the breath, its mind to the synapse, its immune system to the enzyme, its concepts to the percepts, its it to its libido, he meant to take as his geology, structural, historic, and gold-bearing, to locate the gold-bearing rocks, to crush them, to grind them, and to separate out the gold by gravity, by density, by distillation, and by furnace, by in other words, the forces of earth, water, air, and fire. What he would do with that gold, he proposed to let the interaction between himself and society in the market place decide just as he had done with the gold that he literally mined.

To start with, he changed the name of his Company from BRANDON GOLD MINES to BRANDON GOLD MINES AND JEWELRY. Gold mining secured him access to many kinds of people and experiences, but what happened to that gold? He went into partnership with a brilliant Bombay woman jeweler who had everything but capital to do her own enterprise on a proper scale. She set up a shop in Paris and London. She had Parsee connections and Jack knew that fire, which was the Parsee prize symbol, was the key to refining gold, that fire had been the key to humanity's succeeding, and that on his many exploration trips, staring into the fire, sitting in front of his tent, had been the source of his happiness, his dreams, his inspirations.

For his new techniques of concentration, meditation, contemplation, and ecstasy to produce gold he needed memory, imagination, and the full range of human experience. Keeping his company operating, successful, and a good place for his employees, would mean a constant monitor on his ground truth sanity. He knew that this ground truth sanity about the world he lived in was the secret to further reality. It was definitely part of reality. He wanted more reality, all of it he could attain, not to trade one sure part for a part forever dubious because of the lack of testing in the market place. The expansion of his company would increase his need for memory. Partnership with the brilliant Bombay beauty would increase his need for imagination. Moving into Paris and London while keeping his Colorado base and she keeping her Bombay connections would increase his possibilities for experience.

He devoted an hour each weekday morning and two hours on Saturday to his intense assaults on contemplative heights. He gave himself six hours a week to read and recapitulate. He developed his intercourse with dreams by recording each vivid and magnetic one that came.

He knew the first step after the Decision, would be that all his thinking had to change. He had to crea te a new mindset.

This new mindset would look at connections and resonances as primary and things and definitives as secondary. He made a trip around the planet to investigate all the uses of gold. Gilded icons, watches, money, spaceships, bricks stacked in vaults against currency failures, solid elegant castings, toilets for a dictator's airplane, wedding rings, nose rings, slave bracelets and anklets, fish hooks, ashtrays, coca holders, sheets, foil, hoards, speculations, investments, legends, stories, myths, crimes, wars, businesses, explorations, sciences, technologies, goldfever, and special items used as the way to achieve mystical reality by schools of alchemists. Under a waterfall in Kalimantan, searching back for the source of Dyak ornament icons in the second Samadhic state, he watched his mindset change. He saw all the water in the waterfall, comets, oceans, clouds, bodies, trees, all in ceaseless movement. Wherever he looked he no longer saw a thing but a signal from some quasi-infinite range of connections. He came to after he knew not how long a time standing under the waterfall, glowing in body and perception. Stunningly he had seen the connections connecting and swirling all together.

Jack flew back to Colorado and traced out every connection he could find with his business. He worked to improve the connections that were or could be a plus for his process. He cut the ones that would be better connected elsewhere. He made new connections. He and Miti became significantly other and he added the Tantric visualizing techniques.

The next period astonished him. He had grown to expect this continued influx and expansion of his life, happiness and understanding. However, his exercises became meaningless to him. His new millions seemed an excrescence of stupid responsibilities. His sexual-romantic energies were torn between Miti and Beverly Hills. Remorse bit into his life. He had changed his way of thinking, but not his way of behaving. First he quit sugar, not out of diet calculations, but one day when he saw his spoon go into a sugar pot, and watched it come out glistening white with quick energy devoid of constructive aspects, he could not take another spoon of it. He could not stand fudge again. He watched how he avoided certain districts in the big cities. One day he walked back of the Gare du Nord, he had told Miti he had to have some time alone, sat down in a little Moroccan café, and drank mint tea. He stopped going to the grand hotels except for business. He found his life simplifying on its own. His body just seemed to say that's enough of that, you've wasted your life enough on that. He had to make an effort to keep up the business. He knew this was a battlefield. He could sell it up and retire. Live in contemplation of the magnificent swirling universe where everything connected. But he couldn't. His vision included action. His behavior was now what was unconnected, dissonant. Finally, he saw the fault line. His athleticism was what his body had turned bitter about, his football, basketball years, his tough-it-all hikes straight-lining it across rugged almost impassable country. Fifty miles in one day one time straight across the Dakota badlands. Fifty miles in one day straight over Arizona basin and ridge. He wanted to dance, not the way he had, hard aggressive

Saturday night sex dancing, but the dancing of forms of beauty and grace. He curved his body this way and that. He remembered Leonardo's Bacchus in the Louvre. The old Jack had thought how obscene, how queer, but now he saw that he himself was really that Bachus and that half his life had been wasted trying to be a satyr. He told Miti and she slipped him some MDMA and took him to an afternoon session with Marie, an avant-garde dancer on the Rue Mouffetard. Tears flowed from his eyes as he began to let himself move, to imitate the bodily freedom of this beautiful dancer.

His remorse ended when he renounced forever forcing his body to endless torture trying to become, he shuddered to remember, "hard as nails", "tough as shit", "leathery", "fit as a fiddle". He started laughing outrageously. Nails bent easily, shit couldn't stay together, fiddles were easily breakable, and leather cracked. He had of course read in his manuals about a stage called austerity, renunciation, asceticism. He remembered Buddha had given it up as hopeless when he stayed in it too long. But he had never thought giving up his athleticism "hard-nosed" "tough guy" attitude would be his asceticism, his renunciation. He had always thought that forcing himself to perform those physical feats was his discipline, his asceticism. Now he saw it for what it was, a jaded voluptuosity of sex-deviated life energy driving the body literally into the ground, exhausted.

Two years passed while he strove to gain detailed knowledge of the cosmic connections of gold, jewelry, atoms, molecules, starry systems, quanta, humanity, and biospheres, and while he rescued his body from an over-muscled, hardened weary robot into a lithe, responsive, apperceptive being. Miti with her full-scale Tantric sessions and Marie with her dance sessions showed him new maps for exploring for this new gold. He hired Marie's Gabonese boyfriend to drum multi-rhythms while they worked.

Miti told him to step in now and again for a big client. Their jewelry business began to enter the top circles of art and society. He made enquiries at his Moroccan café and made sure there was daily fare for a dozen unemployed whom Hassan assured him were connected with the special music and dance in some way or other. Once they invited him to sit with them while the brotherhood did their music. In Colorado he went to the Cheyenne and sat in companionable silence with old men of power until the spirit moved them and one said, "Clare Big Elk is the young man you should take to train in your business." He partook of the peyote ceremony with them in the sacred tepee in the mountains and for the first time in his life drummed and sang his song and felt no fear to show himself to other humans.

Jack knew now what real gold looked and felt like. Real gold was Miti, Marie, Dobu the drummer, Clare Big Elk, Hassan. Real gold was handling Brandon Gold and Jewelry for the benefit of all its connections including himself and nature and cities. Real gold was not being afraid to manifest as a particle of reality. Real gold was how to keep silent and cool about what you ought to keep silent and cool about.

Corduroy Green

November, 1983

The story begins with Corduroy Green grown up to be a lanky long and strong-armed man with keen eyesight, sandy hair, and a soft slightly drooping mustache. He had started working for the summerfolk in their big frame wide porched houses overlooking the beach when he was fourteen.

Corduroy ran errands, cleaned the beach, and did the odd jobs around the York Harbor Reading Society in which no one was ever caught reading. It was a spacious building for parties and get-togethers by the summerfolk and made the fourth point for their life along with their houses, boats, and places on the beach. They could get sociably "lit" there with their gin, scotch, or whiskey.

Corduroy had to go to work early because his mother believed it was right and good to earn your living, and because they needed the money since his father had died and he had a small sister. His mother repaired clothes for the summerfolk. Corduroy applied himself to his shop classes in high school. The only way out he saw for himself from being a lackey to the "well-lit" and politely superior summerfolk was to become a skilled worker, even a technician.

Graduating from high school at eighteen, he went to Boston to get a job the next fall. Before he left, though, he actualized a delirious dream. Out hunting on one of his long treks through the woods, with his prized Marlin 30-30 he had saved a year to get, he saw four bucks. They saw him, but in a state of consciousness and precision that before he had thought was only an almost masturbatory fantasy, he shot and killed all four, the last two in full motion and between the trees. He left them there. It was illegal. It was against his principles. He could not get caught but he would never forget. Every detail of that incredible and deadly performance lived brighter than sunlight in his memory. He knew he was destined for something extraordinary. He had been marked. Since he was not conventionally religious, his mother had been a lukewarm Baptist, and since his act of supernal grace had been criminal to society and rationally unjustifiable to himself, he could not say marked by God, but he did know that he was marked for some uncommon life. That he was no longer a cosmically anonymous winterfolk waiting on the summerfolk.

In Boston that winter, he failed the army physical to his surprise. He had a weakness in his knees. He became a technician setting up microwave towers for remote area telephones.

One day, he was twenty, he went into a little coffee shop in the Back Bay. A guy his own age got up and read poetry to a group of good looking girls and cool guys.

"Yes," the poet read,
"Our generation's going down the asshole,
They all go down the asshole,
But maybe I'll escape
And go up as a howl of the howl
Circling the moon's dead light."

Corduroy had never heard this kind of poetry. Life is earnest, Life is real, were the only lines he remembered. He sat there, silent, tall, with his acquiline nose and blue eyes.

Finally he noticed the girl on the other side of the table gazing at him affectionately. "Wanna get high?" she said.

In the alley, the hashish she put in the little pipe for them to puff made a hit. He was back in the state when he killed the deer.

He looked into her eyes and smiled. He knew he would make the right moves. This place and people were for him.

Two years later, he'd become "Boston's First Hippy Saint." His hair grew down to his shoulders. His winterfolk clothes fitted right into the scene. They liked his leather and his waterproof boots. He had read Ginsberg and Kerouac, and was reading up on the Buddhists. Now he had a name for the deer killing episode and the quick click with the girl, he called it Zen. These must be the states those Buddhists described. They were Beat-ific. You couldn't Beat them.

A dark-eyed black-haired lady in beads took him to her pad and turned him on to DMT. He saw the actual colors, brighter than sun, like his two memories, emerging without content other than random geometries, exploding in his vision. This is the generating source, he told himself, and it's in me just like they wrote. All I have to do is learn how to tap into this on my own. The insight overpowered or concentrated his sexual energy into his goal; he sat entranced in thought in front of the girl until he got up to leave, bowing to her in thanks.

Walking down the streets of the Italian neighborhood back to his pad, suddenly he was surrounded by sport-coated tough guys. "You hippy shit, you been screwing an Italian girl. You gonna pay!" He lifted, automatically, his hand the way he'd learned to do in the Café and groaned, that was not the right move, for sure that was not Zen whatever Zen was.

He felt his stomach fold in, his head snap to the side, himself trying to run, falling over a leg, elbow smashing on the concrete, up, down, up, down, nose splattering, falling down, kicks, up, boots, jeers, hobbling, a corner light, getting away.

"And we'll really get you next time!"

He left America with two thousand dollars he'd squirreled away. He landed in Tangier. He got high, very high, but a one legged black crow saw him a block away, and hopped straight

43

toward him. He saw the crow hop relentlessly toward him, red-eyed, the crow pecked savagely at his boot. "It's the devil," he heard himself cry out, "the devil!'

He ran to the ferry dock and found himself in Ibiza, then Paris, then at the little hotel off the Boul' Mich' then back in New York working for room and board with a nutty inventor on the Lower East Side. The guy was trying to make the perfect chemical to age metal and wood for antique furniture.

He started to paint. He found a topless dancer and moved in with her. He cooked stew for them six days and she made a big dinner once a week. He dreamed of starting all over again. He decided to go to the Dominican Republic. The topless dancer wanted to know how they'd live. She wouldn't go.

Corduroy went down to the inventor's rooms, broke in and found eleven hundred dollars. It wasn't Zen, but it had a thrill to it. The guys walked on the moon, but Corduroy laughed, he was walking on a deadlier planet by far than the moon. The deadliness of the earth was disguised as long as you were blind to all the new life coming on to die.

There was no scene in Dominican Republic like in Back Bay or the Village, but there were certain kinds of action. He saw a slim black girl in shorts that could not get shorter, high heels on straight dancer's legs, embroidered short-sleeved blouse, and a rakish cap. He was having a coffee. He couldn't take his eyes off her. He know this was the fourth time, the deer, the hippie girl, the crow. It was all up for him. He knew she knew all the moves and that he was the deer. He loved it. He ran for his life, but he left a small target in the trees and he knew it. A delicious shuddering vibrated his body.

"You think I'm a whore," she said. "I'm not. Got a coffee for me?"

"What are you?"

She gazed into him and he felt her looting his heart as he had looted the old inventor's rooms.

"I'm a witch," she said, "with two children, two men, and I was a TV producer in Manhattan at twenty-one, and I think you are ready for me."

He knew she spoke the truth. If a witch was a woman who understood the magic of emotions and could make a man feel all his emotions, the ones he knew about and tried to change or repress, and the ones he didn't even know about, and the ones he could have but didn't know how to make himself, but which would be worth his life to experience, then she was a witch. He knew this beautiful insolent delectable mask sitting down beside him was deadly as a mamba, that she could kill him without a qualm with her emotion witchcraft, but he assented to it, he said yes.

He didn't want to be winterfolk or summerfolk, a skilled worker, a beat saint, an avant-garde artist, a successful criminal, a dull expatriate, he didn't want to be any kind of American or European, he wished to feel life, to feel death, to feel whatever he felt about anything and any person and any situation.

They drank their coffee. She got up. "You coming with me or not?"

"Yes," he said, "Yes, I'm coming with you."

She was supported financially by an old man with a cough who drew a big pension from Germany. He couldn't hardly move, but she would dance naked in front of him once a day for three minutes and he could listen to whatever happened with anyone else. Her two children were brilliant and she sent them to special tutors. Her lover Pedro had been a middleweight candidate for the championship, but had his left hand crushed in a gang fight. He was her and her children's devoted protector and occupied the big bed with her. Corduroy was needed for the slave service and handyman skills. He had to run get the cigarettes or the beer. She would walk with him to the art galleries and to the plaza coffee shops, and take a nighttime stroll with him before going to bed. Once a week she made love to him. She would always say, "I hope Pedro doesn't kill you for this." He was deathly afraid that Pedro would.

She jacked the old man off once a week.

She had a small clientele. He asked her what witches did. "They give people experiences they would never get anywhere else."

"Does it do them any good?"

"Does it do you any good? Or bad? Experience is life itself."

This was beyond the Zen he read about, this experience. Maybe there were other things in other teachings, certain words that might conceal some reality he should know like wisdom or history or peacefulness or longevity, but he wanted, was mad for these experiences she gave, these feelings of terror, horror, emptiness, disbelief, mockery, insanity, impossibility, jealousy, comprehension.

Of course he had run out of money. He lived on the scraps she fed him. "Slaves aren't worth that much, you know," she said.

He stopped maintaining the house. The septic tank overflowed and smelled. He slowpoked his way to get cigarettes or beer. Pedro slugged him to teach him a lesson.

After three years he fell ill. A quick acting cancer. "I'll throw you on the street," she said. "You did it to yourself. You are not going to spoil my children's life."

He begged an air ticket from his mother. He went back home to die. Four deer dead in seconds. The extraordinary café love affair. His direct contact with the super sunlight and being beaten on the street. The black crow. Stealing freedom from the old inventor. Feeling everything a man could feel with the black witch.

A Wandering Minstrel

January, 1980

When the moon turned to cheese again
My aching became a hounddog grin
I turned into a cliché clown
To take off this kinky town.
I descended into creepy crawly sadness
Till I met you, your gawky badness
Grooved me into cool cool madness.
Yeah! I tore like Coltrane into my guitar
Ate up that cheesy moon, became a star,
Now you and I roam gun-spattered night
But that's allright, allright?
Because you and I know damn well
Life's no pearl-picking wishing well
So wander on come what may
Through breathless dark to breathing day.

B ob Addison wandered the poetry reading cafés of Canada and the United States for twenty years. He attended nearly all the neo-tribal gatherings and the big events like the great Be-In that opened up 1967 in San Francisco. His aim was to stay free, spend a lot of time in wilderness, become the victor over both solitude and crowd, and to pay for his food, travel, loves, and helping friends by giving musical pleasure laced with a few agenbites of inwit.

A tall rangy guy with long arms, whip-muscled shoulders, big feet and bony knees, he peered through his large wide-eyebrowed eyes set into an angular face surrounded by long blonde hair, occasionally gathered back into a ponytail, especially when on his solitary treks through the Wind River Range, the Bitterroots, or the hot Pinotecs just south of the Arizona border with Mexico. Every two or three years he would take off to canoe and fish in the northern Ontario lakes. Every five years he'd go hang out in Jaguar jungle in Belize. He never skied at a resort, only cross-county in the winter on occasion with a Swedish friend in Northern Michigan, sometimes with a couple of girls from Iron Mountain.

Bob had memorized three books, Walt Whitman's *Song of the Open Road* and *Song of Myself* and Lao Tse's *Tao Te Ching*. He read the New York Times, when he got hold of it, from front to back including the ads, maybe a dozen times a year. "That's all I need to read except the four classic books: nature, people, sky, and earth". He was a great listener whether with his ear on the ground, or his ears located on a safe bough on strategic tree, or from a slightly bent head over an intimate table or beside a fire. Bob loved stories. He thought stories transmitted knowledge better than anything.

In 1978, Bob turned forty and realized that he would die someday. He'd thought the Vietnam War the dumbest thing the United States had ever gotten into, though he had no objection to fighting any invader, and so he had avoided being drafted by faking an all-out S & M homosexual trip at his examination. But it wasn't that he was scared of dying. Intellectually, of course, he recognized that he could and very probably would die like everyone else, but emotionally he never felt it. He was too healthy, smart and lucky. He even laughed at himself on occasion for feeling immortal, but he couldn't deny it, he did feel immortal. He liked the feeling because it gave him all the time in the world. His contemporaries grew flaccid, tied to a wife and mortgage, slave laborers to machine and profit calculations, less and less able to survive outside a society that tied them down to its rigorous aging, disease, and dying schedules.

He got caught in an early blizzard in the San Juan Mountains at over ten thousand feet, in his pup tent for four days.

He could barely snowshoe out and down to his pickup. It had fallen to thirty below zero. He'd used every trick he knew to stay alive.

But not until he lazed into the Slater Hotel in Durango to his favorite old table for stew and a cup of coffee did it hit him. Looking around at all those soft-faced soft-minded people, he realized that they all felt they were immortal, that death was somebody else's funeral they'd attend to be polite, that his cherished imaginary world that had made him feel so elite was everybody's cherished imaginary world. They didn't give a rat's ass what they did because they had all the time in the world, anymore than he did. Because he lived in the wilderness where one had to stay alert to stay alive and because he wandered through strange cities and strange cultures where he also had to be observant and quick or go to jail or get beat up or robbed, and because he was always having to make new friends and girls in new places and even in old places because past friends and girls had disappeared down the local cultural time sequence, he had to keep flexible and responsive. So he had thought that this difference must go all the way to the core, to his central unique fantasy. No, he now realized, our central fantasy is the same, we all think we're going to live forever, and that's how I just about took one chance too many, staying up there with a falling barometer, thinking it's too early in the fall to get really bad, and they stay on their routine, thinking it's too early in the fall to get really stuck..

He drove on down to Cuba in New Mexico to see an old beautiful woman he had fallen madly in love with at an exhibition of her paintings in Albuquerque. She was in her eighties and her eyes were as vast and mysterious as the New Mexico skies which were why she'd said she'd moved there from her famous studio in Manhattan. "Because I know I'd never be able to paint it, but that's what I wanted to spend my life endeavoring to do."

"Georgia," he said to her, after she'd fixed them up a pot of tea and they sat down on her sun-splattered patio, but then he couldn't continue. He looked into her eyes and she looked into his. Mask after mask seemed to drop. He saw death masks, disease masks, love masks, ambition masks, power masks, finally he saw the mask maker and then he saw, and it was realer than blood to him, and he didn't care whether his critical intellect called it fantasy, revelation, or ultimate defense mechanism or whatever, it was realer than food to his feeling that she and he and all the people at the Slater Hotel and the Seri Indians and the hair-raising grizzly and the eye-raising yellow pines and the sex-raising blonde girls at the poetry cafes and his arm-raising young canoers in Canada and this mind-raising wonder of an old woman mask maker were each Masks of a great Masked Being. So, he would never die, but keep making masks because the pure light unmasked would blind and destroy the Universe. Bob Addison would be his Mask until that light began to melt away. Then he would make a good bye Mask for Bob, Bob's death mask, and make himself a new Mask that would fool even an electron microscope checking it out, that it was really just a human.

He and Georgia smiled affectionately at each other, at last breaking eye contact, and holding each other's hands, transmitting each insight as it came by the smallest change of pressures.

Bob pondered, weighed out his thoughts and feelings as he drove south to do a reading in Tucson, then one in Mexico City, and then, hopefully, continue on down with one of those new independent Mexican ladies (now they were a great new set of Mask-makers) to do his first diving adventure in the deep coral reef atolls off Belize. He felt he could dive down deep now as well as climb up high.

Bob liked his new story. The gray-eyed anthropologist from Harvard he'd met at Hovenweep five years ago would call it his personal myth and say softly to him in that heart-breaking Four Corners moonlight as she had once whispered other secrets of human science to him that "real truth can never be known by the human mind, so science is ultimately unsatisfactory to the human heart, and so every culture has its myths that reconcile its people to the facts of life."

But probably all myths started as somebody's personal myth. Some myths would satisfy others, from one other to several million. They all had to finally become someone's personally accepted myth. Bob was happy to have come up with his own. He knew, at last he had come down with the Indians and the ancients, that the heart was the center of the human being, not the head, and his heart had its own good reasons for its truth. Let his head sneer all it wished, that "You've just accepted a lie in order not to face death and to stay happy until you can't escape reality when your throat is choking."

A brilliant old brujo had once told him after getting him to drink some datura tea that death flew like a valiant eagle at his shoulder and that he should prepare himself to wage to the full his last warrior's combat, dying proudly, impeccably, dancing.

But now he sensed only his heart expanding, sensed his arteries, his veins, his body pulse following the beat, the small distributed pressure of the capillaries, he "saw" the blood, its ever-changing chemicals turning on, turning off, changing, tuning up the nerves that operated his muscular responses to incoming energies transformed into color, sound and touch indicators. And operating this great heart he felt contact with the contemplator, the Great Masked Being, who could use anything as its mask, and his heart finished his story for him, "You are a masked scout for that, what you used to call Tao or Song of the Open Road, and when you come back with your report you will be sent out again to a greater or lesser scouting expedition depending on the interest of what you find."

Now he was really hot to get to Tucson, to Mexico City, to the Blue Hole. What would he find there? He was ready, forever ready.

A Woman Who Left

May, 1982

Edie May liked to think of herself as a Southern Girl from the time she turned twelve years old. Big gold-flecked blue eyes, that tell-tale slimness that showed she would stay slim her entire life, a sharp-edged energy, clever long fingers, small feet, smart, tough, and she liked men, liked them so much that she knew exactly which poses they wished to see her assume, that's what she admired in herself as a Southern girl. She would've gotten along great in the old old South playing croquet, dancing, riding, reading Sir Walter Scott, and dealing with her beaux. And in her old South there would've been no slaves. No, the cotton gin would not have been invented, slavery would have died out, unprofitable, as Jefferson and Washington had projected, and the South would have raised crops like cattle and corn, but with the style of life-loving Cavaliers not moralizing grungy Northern Puritans.

Edie May was bright and she'd started thinking and reading for herself at ten years old. She felt capable and she loved to flirt. That was part of the best of being a Southern Girl. In high school she loved to sit in the porch swing and make out in the jasmine laden summer night with her steady of the moment. But she would always have his replacement in sight the moment he faltered in romance. It was clear to her and everyone that she would go on to college and become a Phi Beta Kappa as well as a Lambda Chi, and after a dazzling year or two in New York in publishing or something take a leisurely trip to Europe and then find her man.

Except at eighteen, her first year at Georgia University, she fell head over heels and lock stock and barrel for Jim Farnsworth, son of the very rich Farnsworth family, although his father wasn't as rich as his brothers. Edie May married him her freshman summer, and dropped out of college her sophomore summer to have a baby, and a second baby came when she was twenty-one. Jim joined up with the Hippies and they moved to the one hot spot in the region, near The Armadillo, where occasionally legends of San Francisco or New York came by but the locals made a far-out scene of it all the time anyway, because they weren't famous and weren't going to get famous, so they couldn't just go through the motions. Jim and some others did get a certain notoriety in the area though.

One day police kicked down the door of their little house and found Jim with a long slim pipe, happily stoned. Edie May was already in a blissful state, and having just put the children to sleep, sat romantically at Jim's feet. Suddenly he was shaken, handcuffed and tossed in jail. His family sprang him the next day, but Jim and Edie May were both terrified and furious. They split the state and began to wander, finally joining a commune in Oregon.

There they both found they were quite attractive to the opposite sex, and before long he had an affair, which she topped, and then it became a race. After a year she went off with a young Frenchman, toured Morocco with him, and passed three months in Tangier, in the mountains, on the Southern coast, all in a Berber's magic spell hinting of emotions and states that aroused an inner calm in her like an eye in a hurricane. She and the Frenchman broke up in Nice, but she sent for the two children and became the manager of an American school's property near Montpellier. Her French had become quite impeccable since passion had made it interesting. Victor Hugo and Anatole France replaced Sir Walter Scott, but then she went to Avignon experimental theater festivals and met bi-sexy intellectuals who showed her how to deconstruct texts of books she had considered "sacred", like the U.S. Constitution, the Bible, the Koran, Macbeth, to demonstrate the different quite non-sacred interests being catered to by this carefully edited section and that carefully truncated section. She even deconstructed "The Southern Girl," a non-textual oral tradition, laughing Rabelaisianly as the meanings of each mince, stare, pause, and curl became all so clear.

She lost faith in her 141 I.Q., her score on an American test of middle class intelligence that she had believed certified her "a genius" because the people giving the test had said so. She realized how she didn't really know much of anything except how to get laid, have children, take care of them, get high, and have what seemed to be sparkling intense intellectual conversations in two languages that wound up showing that in all probability there was no such "thing" as truth, only a rhetoric designed to defend or attack a position based on a will or at least an instinct to power.

The young Americans who came over didn't really interest her, though she had a couple of flings. Bright, shiny faces, seeing a few months in France as a great career move, a "time-out" before job and marriage, or just simply as prestigious. They hung out together like a pack and constantly scrutinized each other's comings and goings. Occasionally a Frenchman would dive in and pick up one of the girls.

One day she drove to Marseilles to get away from her job, the kids, now seven and five, and the surveillance of Montpellier where she was now known to all sorts of observers of the scene. She had had a one month affair with a notorious Sapphic who taught her the underground criminal slang, the *argot*, which she delighted in putting into her conversations with the local bourgeois, together with the local accent. She began to raise eyebrows and chins and to tighten the lower lips in many of the French social figures. Her boss received for the first time questions about her from the Prefect and the Priest. He tried to joke with her about it so she would rein herself in a little, "at least the third of the unholy triangle, the Notary, hasn't yet said anything." But it was now too easy for her to deconstruct his conversation and see exactly what was being threatened and by whom and for what. So now she walked up from the Inner Harbor, beneath the soaring cathedral with all its models of shipwrecks on the peak behind toward the Mediterranean, past the ruins of the vibrant Greek metropolis destroyed by the efficient, technically brilliant, unimaginative Romans, on up the long rise into little Africa where she wanted to have a nostalgic couscous and mint tea, to remember a certain numinous glamour she had experienced in Morocco. Was it only sex and hashish, or had there really been something in that culture that had bespoken deep wisdom, how to live one's life moment by moment, yet in harmony with the entire experience of a people some six thousand years old? Something that couldn't be deconstructed or hallucinated?

At the small café with its small wooden tables and chairs, practically the same as many she had sipped tea in during her Moroccan adventure, she slowly slipped into a reverie in which she saw the scenes of her life slipping by like a long wall of paintings, each a creation of memory, each now devoid of meaning to anyone but herself, doomed to be destroyed when death burnt down her museum. At twenty-seven, she was as good as dead. She would have to go back to Montpellier, apologize, change her behavior, keep the job at all costs even if only to get the chance at a better one, suck up to people, pretend to be what she was not. All of her options passed quickly before her eyes. She had to bring up her two children, she would never abandon them, but as middle class Americans or intellectual French? She smiled an amusement that surprised herself with its detached, almost Olympian self-mockery.

A lean Moroccan sat down by her, his big workman's hands with their strong square fingernailed fingers clasped together in a relaxed way on the table in front of him. He glanced at her merrily.

"You have just won the battle with your memories. I was watching you. You are a very strong as well as beautiful woman."

She looked at his strong nose, his laughing brown eyes, his blue workshirt with a red neckerchief.

"I want some good couscous," she said.

"Come with me. I take you to my cousin's. He makes the best."

After that day, she came back to Marseilles every weekend for the next three weeks, the last two with her children. Hamid had taken to them. He took Edie and them to his family's small house. She enjoyed the great gatherings of twenty-odd people, guests dropping by.

They were all working people and wanted to be working people except two of the young ones in high school, one of whom wanted to be a scientist and one a dancer. They expressed their emotions, did not deconstruct anything, accepted life, work, struggle, limitations, dreams, not being geniuses, and joked about people's shortcomings. They formed a sort of a caravan moving through life, a caravan following a definite route, moving through country interesting to her.

Hamid belonged to a brotherhood of singers. Women were allowed only to watch. She was fascinated and then made extremely happy watching Hamid and his brothers sing under the subtle direction of their leader. She suddenly realized it was the first time on her life she was happy because someone else was happy. And Hamid was happy because his brotherhood was happy. A great secret disclosed itself to her.

That night, locked in embrace, he told her his teacher said she was a good woman. "That means I can marry you!"

"I'm not a Moslem, I'm an independent woman."

"You are a good woman, only you are not so happy. I am in France, not Morocco. I was born here. You can help manage my family's restaurant. There is no harem here. We are a new kind of people."

Shortly after that, she left her apartment and job, silently, at night, without notice. She had two more children and said, "Enough!"

She became the family's advisor on matters financial and legal. She helped make the restaurant into a place where many people could eat and dream. "Actually, it's only one of the places we can live," she laughed to a French intellectual who questioned her why she was in Little Africa, when 'a woman like you could be in Paris or New York.' "Maybe instead of Little Africa as you call us, it's a Big Dream, and if it's a dream, let's live as we really wish, so that if we do wake up and out of the dream, we'll have practiced how to keep the action going."

A Man Who Wanted To Be a Scientist

June, 1977

Darley wanted to be a scientist so badly that he did a thousand crazy things. As a college sophomore he had entered a room in which Enrico Fermi was holding the audience hypnotized, in the palms of his wondrous voice. "You ask how could I be so confident that the atomic reactor would work when I showed it for the first time in that Chicago tennis court? I knew," Fermi laughed a polyphrenic laugh that showed Darley that here a master magician was playing with the audience of professors, engineers, financiers, and a couple of gate crashers like himself, "because, although we all swore not to go back till morning's public experiment when we stopped our work for the day, I got up in the middle of the night and said, I have to know before anyone else, and since I had the key, I sneaked in and pushed the uranium rod, it worked, I drew it out, and so next morning, I was very confident."

Darley wanted to do that and be that. Do something that changed the world and be the man who could expound the real truth behind how the change occurred. Fermi had shown him the way, this Italian fighter against dictatorship. Before, he had wanted to be an actor. But what would he have acted, Hamlet or Man and Superman (the two plays that had turned him on)? Now he knew what role he wanted to act, right on the stage of life. A great scientist.

He got out of classics, speech, and history immediately and enrolled in anthropology, the science of humanity. Obviously less was known here than in physics when Fermi started. He would discover the atomic energy of humanity.

It was clear to Darley, inductively speaking, that sex was the atomic energy of humanity. What was its formula? The Incest Taboo! You shall not fuck your mother! Armed with this No the mass of Humanity accelerated to explode into kinship systems, aim-displaced creative energy, invention and aggression. Had anybody gone around to test this hypothesis? Sophocles (a playwright) had shown that Oedipus got more energy than anyone else in Thebes by fucking his mother and killing his father. No one had set up any experiments, nor even tried to find all the motherfuckers to see what happened to that population. People laughed as if he were making a joke when he proposed it. It. Experimental motherfucking was a discussion taboo! Darley had made his great anthropological discovery. There was always something that could not be discussed in every culture. This Accelerated Mass of Humanity Could be Controlled by Discussion Taboo. The Free Speech amendment to the American constitution did not mean this taboo could be violated.

Darley was told brusquely to go into archeology, that he was not a real scientist, but a troublemaker. He needed the discipline of real facts. Going to Cholula in Mexico, he saw a great Spanish cathedral on top of a much greater Indian pyramidal colossus. "What an excrescence! Why isn't that removed, that insult to the Indians?"

"Oh, there's one on top of nearly every Indian site in the Americas and pagan site in Europe."

"Now that's an archeology paper. I'll make a study and put out a book of the Catholic Church's slaughter of local religions and putting up their churches in detail, mapping out its exact time progress of conquest."

"Darley, you're not really an archeologist, we're looking for ancient burials, by which we mean before the Spanish killings, in this old artificial mountain. It's using a fine brush and patience that are required. You're just not a scientist."

So he became a chemist to do some "hard" science. He soon created a molecule. A phenylethylamine, that could produce most of the effects of LSD but lasted only four hours. He had found a secret to making a population of drugs whose effects could be carefully studied to determine the best with least side effects for the aim taken. This he found out, as the armed officer knocked in his lab door, was not only taboo, but criminal. This science which intensely interested some hundreds of millions of intelligent people around the planet was to be crushed in its entirety by decree from an armed agency.

Realizing from his anthropological studies of monotheist ruthlessness, animist cruelty, polytheist sacrifices, and state murderousness that going through this closed door would be fatal even to a Fermi, he slobbered, begged, smashed up his lab, apologized, swore he'd seen the light, and was only jailed for two days, fined heavily, given a record, and humiliated and handcuffed. But nothing would stop Darley from his obsession to become like Fermi, a great scientist, a fighter against tyranny, a burst of laughter in the gloom.

Ecology, the science of life systems, seemed in trouble to Darley, open to a new discovery or two. Controversy raged over every one of its findings. The problem, Darley announced at a meeting he'd managed to sneak into after two years reading his Margalef and Odum, and buying ten acres of marshland to observe and measure, was that Heisenberg's uncertainty principle worked not only on systems like photons much smaller than scientists, but on ecosystems, much bigger than scientists. The uncertainty was exactly the same, whatever the scientist measured, that's what he got within the limits of manifestation of the forms: wave or particle for the photon, population or community of biome or biosphere or... or ... for the ecologist. It was scientists changing their mind not the X or Y changing that changed their answer. So which answer is most useful of the possible ones should be the approach in both physics and ecology. And most useful would depend upon the results to humanity and the biosphere, he announced.

Darley was barred from all future meetings of ecologists and from all ecologist-controlled publications. His name was simply not mentioned. "We're scientists, we don't beat people up, we simply make them look like jackasses," wise-laughed the Society's president. "Then they come to their senses or disappear into the woodwork, kooks who don't get the paradigm, freaks who don't submit to the butt-spanking of their peers, and get the freedom of us initiates to run around in disguises that don't rock an important boat."

Darley decided to make another try. He was very inspired by Fermi, how Fermi had overcome Mussolini's put-downs, how Galileo had survived the Church's Inquisition, by all that wonderful mythology of science, that he was certain was true, because otherwise, he couldn't have seen Fermi do it. But he was now also certain there were good reasons why anyone could count up the number of scientists who had made any real science on their fingers and toes. Who were all the rest of those people calling themselves scientists? Who were all these people calling themselves actors, mystics, leaders, lovers and so on. That something was so rare and valuable that counterfeits flourished only made it the more desirable. "Ah-hah," said Darley, "another discovery!"

Darley realized he had become a very famous scientist to himself. Fermi, he recalled, only became famous because 'they' were building an atomic bomb, Darwin because 'they' were building a 'survival of the fittest engine', called an Empire, Fraser because 'they' were building a culture that 'they' wanted to be supreme over all others, Freud because 'they' were building such an insane society 'they' had to know what people's subconscious was thinking, Egyptian pyramid and Indian tomb engineers, because 'they' wanted to establish a line of tradition 'they' descended from, a line sanctified by greater architecture than that built by the conquered.

Darley decided to become a real scientist, non-famous, who truly could think freely and many-sidedly, and let out only what he knew when he had eliminated the part that violence and profiteering could use.

Darley was then proclaimed not only non-scientist, but an anti-scientist for refusing to publish his important discoveries that could be of so much use to his suffering fellow humans if only he hadn't selfishly kept them for himself.

Darley made a pilgrimage to the window of the room where Tesla died after his favorite white pigeon stopped visiting him. Tesla had destroyed all evidence of his powerful new inventions. Humanity was not yet ready for more knowledge was Tesla's verdict, or if it was, its rulers certainly weren't. But Tesla himself had continued and enjoyed his wild electrical experiments.

Darley found ever new subjects for a scientist to study. Silence, Inscrutability, Enigma, History and Hope. He had finally to smile at himself and his endless discoveries of important facts. He had been as stupid in his way as the head of the Ecological Society. He strolled down to Little Italy to have a good wine, lasagna and expresso. He felt at last ready to study existences, real science, real knowing, and stop being a wise-ass.

The Artist Who Gave Up
On Artists

April, 1980

A tall corn-shocked beauty with a small butterfly tattooed on the rear of her slim left ankle, Sandy Mara was born back of the steel mills in Pueblo, Colorado, half Mexican, half Irish. Discovered in high school when she submitted a sculpture in the state contest, she won a scholarship to Denver University in the Arts.

No doubt about it, on graduation she would be headed for the Village to make her try in New York. While at Denver, though, she danced every Saturday night at a Denver or Colorado University or Colorado Mines party, specializing in glueing her pelvis to the man's, leaning back from her waist and gazing with great green eyes at him or else whispering sweet intimations while she whirled merrily away. Sex and brains, she wanted them both at the same time. Every month or two she made it big in a motel to keep herself in energetic balance, but she always switched boyfriends, three or four a year during her junior and senior years. She had gone to a good gynecologist and gotten a good diaphragm. She hated putting it in, but felt she didn't want to slow up the guy once he turned on. She drank a couple of glasses of wine at her dances and her events as she called the special nights.

Sandy went through her Giacometti and then her Brancusi and then her Matisse phases. She studied the modern masters from Rodin onward. Before Rodin she felt there had been ideals or ideas sculpted, or stories, but not the direct expression of total feeling. To be sure, she acknowledged, she had not been to Italy to see directly the later Michelangelos. Sandy got into stainless steel, polished interlooping surfaces, complex to see but kinesthetically thrilling and self-explanatory to touch. You don't need eyes to see my sculpture, she would slyly joke, only Eros.

She won a couple of prizes plus her scholarship so she had paid eighty percent of her costs, living frugally in a two room apartment with a girl studying forestry. Her family made up the rest. Occasionally, she took her father's old Ford pickup to camp out with her friend, grokking the shapes of pines, spruce, birch, cottonwoods, changing their mighty volumes in her imagination to the three foot scale she liked best to work with. Her friend on the other hand would take a leaf and a root and produce a thousand square mile biome in her mind. Art and Science, Mara said, art concentrating the general to the particular and science generalizing the particular to the universal. The thing was, she also said, science nearly always interested her, even its mistakes, while even good scientists usually bored her; art except when it "worked" bored her, but even a lousy artist sometimes interested her.

She knew she had to meet and live closely with real artists. That's why she wished to go to New York. She knew she would become the lover of some real artists there. She had a just appraisal of the power of her twenty-one year old beauty from her dozen or so experiments with athletes, young assistant professors, and musicians. But she wished to have her emotions, her reactions, her cool tested and sculpted to a tensile strength that would carry her through a long creative life. She figured she had five charmed years of nubility to invest in gaining quick personal experience of the world of artists. She thought it almost unfair that she would be able to enter those circles of achievers easier than a young guy of the same ability. All she need do would be not to fall madly in love, but intelligently, and to move on when he or she had reached the end of what they had to give each other. Later she realized certain kinds of young guys could make the same rapid entry.

As it happened, she found and fell for two artists at the same time, one a young writer, who came in and out of the Village from California, and the other, an older painter too scandalous for her Cedar Street crowd of abstract expressionists, or even Warhol. He flew in from time to time from Paris to sell his richly finished superb oil paintings to a special uptown clientele. She met Jackson, the painter, one Saturday at the San Remo.

She had taken up a station at the bar, where she could track the bar crowd, the table scenes, and the entries through the swinging door. She coolly sipped her glass of red wine.

Jackson, white-haired, lithe, sharp-eyed, with an open throat shirt and soft suede jacket, locked into her eyes immediately.

He left open a window in his Chelsea apartment onto the walled ground floor garden outside the old brick row house. An early fall mist entered the small bedroom with stout oaken bed. She had never seen paintings like his. She understood immediately why he sold, why his work was not hung in museums, why the artistic and critical elite knew and respected his name. He painted surrealist vivid incredibly colored sex canvases, each one an idea about sex that expressed itself without let or hindrance. He had just finished one before going to the San Remo. "I had painted you," he said, "and then I went looking for you. You had to exist because my vision of you was so complete." The "ontological argument," he laughed at himself after a moment.

The painting was of a nude full-length girl amazingly like herself, even to the color of skin, eyes and hair, stretched out in total revelry of her arcane mastery of each subtle ligament on a background of mauve with not a single line, simply pure color. The girl was besieged by a hundred penises, each different, each attacking a different yielding of the musculature. Huge darts, each different, each fully detailed, and she the object of the tournament. Where was the bull's eye? Or was each place a transcendent hit?

He took her to Carnegie Hall, to the stacks of hidden paintings and sculpture at the Museum of Modern Art, let her watch him paint a model, then she modeled for him. She sat with him when he showed and sold his work. The one of you before I met you, though, he said, is yours.

She met the young writer at the Kiwi, a hardcore breakaway crowd from the San Remo, located below street level on Houston Street, filled with merchant seaman who'd read their B. Traven, Iroquois high-rise workers, hard drinking Irish writers or would-be writers who thought the White Horse too pretentious, and adventurous girls from certain Ivy League Upper East Side set who passed on the Kiwi to a special friend when they graduated.

He took her to meet Albee who placed his hand on his stack of Camus, Ionesco, and Beckett like they were bibles, and to see his plays, the Zoo Story and the American Dream. Jeff came out of that play so charged he set off running down the village streets, she racing after. Jeff wrote in a pad in Little Italy on Mott Street. "Only the Mafia keeps crime away in the city," he joked.

She would sit up till midnight with him while he and his Hungarian poet friend dissected their latest poems, word by word, phrase by phrase, line by line, stanza by stanza, punctuation mark by punctuation mark. A bottle of Chianti and a ball of mozzarella cheese formed the backbone of his sustenance, together with fruit, raw vegetables, and when he was feeling romantic, a steak with bacon and raspberries to cut the bacon's fat, he explained.

Neither of them ever asked her if he were her only lover. Each of them gave and took her total attention while they were on. She, an independent beautiful young woman who could listen, interact, groove, appreciate, make love and be available two or three times a week, seemed to fulfill their needs, their imaginations. She understood that. She didn't want to complicate her life into being bourgeois, either.

She began to play with found objects, tires slashed in long ribbons, piano keys found jumbled up with broken strings, a baseball bat with a hole drilled through its head and a gold bracelet around its hold. She visualized her body being worked by the painter into outlines, colors, textures, gaps, connections, and by the writer into metaphor, synecdoche, dialectic, and free association.

She began to see how artists lived and worked, how she herself made convexes, concaves, planes, ledges, voids, clay, marble, and steel out of her lovers.

After a year, Jackson trotted in from Paris, to tell her he was dying of cancer. He had little money. He'd spent as he earned. She, un-asked, swore to take care of him until he died.

Jeff wanted her to go to the Bitter Root Mountains for a month to work with a Crow shaman. She said she couldn't. She could not believe his amazed uncomprehending look or the vicious way he said "Fuck you, then!"

"I'll be able to later," she said.

"There's no later in art," he flung back. "It's always Now or Never. I know you got somebody else. That's why you're not coming."

"He's dying. He's a great artist. He's lonely. He's miserable. He's frightened."

"Today you choose between life and death," he yelled. After Jackson died, she moved back into her two rooms she shared with another girl who studied acting and waited tables.

Mara thought over Jackson and Jeff for two months, what she had learned about artists. What it meant to her.

It came to her that in the thirteenth century in Chartres, or the seventh century in the Byzantium, or possibly even in 1900 Paris and a dozen other historical times, that she would continue with Art, with its eternities to play with Illusion and Reality to express the passions that must be expressed or die slowly within.

But since it was not such an age, she decided to live and breed for the future when the worship of beauty would recur. Return to the Rockies and find a good genetic masterpiece with a good productive mind and skilled hands, a rancher or a maker of projects. She would of course, continue to create sculpture, a home, a garden, a cuisine, a way of life. That she could and would do, put art deeply into her life, but not her life deeply into art as art was today, the today of her youth.

She cried long and bitterly. She packed all her tools and clothes in a workman-like manner. She left New York on the train, to make what she could with what she had and what would happen to her and what she would find. Besides Art and Science, History also had its say about what you could achieve.

An Actress from Brooklyn

June, 1984

This story begins with: Maud Halloran's mother, Kathleen, who was an undercover cop, tall, and not beautiful, but overall gorgeous, or as her fellow cops called her, a knockout. Her face did not stand up to examination for beauty, but her fluid movements made her into a "fine figure of a woman" to all who beheld her. Her specialty was impersonating prostitutes and booking the naïve John .

Divorced from her broad-shouldered beefy husband, who had moved into the Jersey union office, she reared three children in her two bedroom Brooklyn apartment. She enlarged a closet for the boy. Maud, the eldest, was her favorite. Kathleen thought Maud was truly beautiful and had a real personality. Kathleen was determined to get Maud into the movies.

When Maud turned fourteen, Kathleen started taking her once a month to see a hit movie. After, they would go to the Russian Tearoom on 57th next to Carnegie Hall. "This is where the producers come," she whispered to Maud. "And the directors. I want you to get used to this place and look like you're part of it. Observe how these people behave. Use clues like I do in my detective work. Pick up on how they dress, walk, laugh, learn to see who's the boss. You're going to get discovered here by the time you're sixteen."

Maud spent hours in the bathroom in front of the full length mirror her mother had specially bought for her, practicing postures, eye movements, facial expressions, make-up and costume. With disdain, she avoided high school drama classes.

Her father tried to gain his share of her attention when he realized what was going on. He drove by to get her for the three times that Roethlisberger showed up at the union hall to paint his action abstractions. Maud picked up some of the form language, but most of all the body language of the art crowd. The stark black and whites on the canvases trained her eye. Mostly she was attracted by the sex energy flowing from the art crowd. She knew they were sleeping with each other. She was fifteen and excited by their freedom. The last art party took place just before she was sixteen. She really turned on to a curly, black-haired Jewish guy, a live wire who was himself a painter. He took her out the backdoor into the alley and soon had her roused to a tumult. An idea struck her.

"Come to my apartment on the evening of my birthday next week."

It was a night her mother worked. She and Maud would lunch at the Russian Tearoom. Go to an afternoon movie, then Maud would go home, make supper, put the two young ones to bed, and wait for him.

She had found some sleeping pills in her mother's cabinet. She dumped a good dose in the glasses of milk she set out for the children. Then she tucked them into bed.

Moisheh arrived and Maud spurred him on. She was eager to find out all about it, to liberate her energies, to make her body knowledgeable about life. She needed to be ready when the right producer smiled at her.

The next week at the Russian Tearoom, Maud stretched languidly beside Kathleen, who was struck by the new self - confidence of her daughter. A party of Japanese were in an animated conversation two tables away. The boss, or center of the party at least, gave her the eye. She gave him half an eye back, just enough to start the current.

A minute later she turned her green eyes back in his direction and caught him in full glance. Her mother had noticed and excused herself to go to the toilet. The Japanese got up and approached her when her mother had disappeared. He produced a card. "My name is Hiromoto."

She knew who he was. The hottest avant-garde filmmaker in town. Shown at the Museum of Modern Art. Her mother gave her a full briefing on who came to the tearoom. She lowered her head slightly. Her chin was a bit too long. Her only flaw to the camera. She used her eyes and nose, her best three-quarters profile.

Yes, she studied acting. Yes, she would come by his place in two days to see if she might be the one for his new film about a lonely, ambitious girl who was lost in her dreams. "About what?" "Theater of Cruelty." The film would show this young girl discovering exactly what the Theater of Cruelty meant.

He rose as her mother came back and bowed nicely to her as he returned to his table. "Yes, he asked me for an audition," she whispered. "That's good," her mother smiled. "His films don't make money, but the others," she glanced around significantly, "go to see them, and if they like the actress ..."

When she showed up at his apartment in the Chelsea, he introduced her to his smiling appraising wife and then took her upstairs to his studio. They were alone. There were no nude scenes, but one scene was essential that she be bare breasted. If she could let him see. Unfortunately, not many girls had breasts that matched their face, aesthetically-speaking of course.

She slipped off her blouse and skirt to stand in her leotards and turned this way and that as he indicated while he shifted positions. He liked her deadpan face and insolent eyes, the ratio of the long round arms and short round breasts; the slightly long chin suited his satirical mind. They kept moving around each other for an hour.

"Come back in two days. I'll show you some of my work and if we hit the next stage in rapport, we'll start shooting. " He tossed her Artaud's *Theater of Cruelty* to read. "The girl I'm portraying lives by herself with a mother that's gone most of the time. She daydreams in school of being a great and famous actress. She wants to be something new. She believes that cruelty to her beliefs, her habits, her dreams will be the catalyst that will make her real self bloom."

The next time she came, his wife was gone. He showed her a film of a Japanese boy being ridiculed, made to work like a slave, running away, picked up for a lover by a rich man, running away, wandering through thousands of cherry blossoms which suddenly became faces falling and then back to cherry blossoms being walked upon carelessly by the rich man and the man who had ridiculed him. The intelligent face of the boy glowed as he watched the cherry blossoms being crashed beneath the careless feet.

"The secret of my films is my rapport with the main actor. I am not proposing to be your lover, but we should spend the afternoon knowing each other intimately, and to do that we must act this once as lovers."

She had great hopes of special oriental secrets, but the afternoon disappointed her, though she made as sure as she could it did not disappoint Hiromoto.

He arranged to pay her two thousand dollars plus supply all her meals, transport, all her costume and make-up, explaining avant-garde films were low budget, but she would get five per cent of any profit. She was certain she would at last learn real secrets of art. Her mother thought for sixteen it was a good start.

In the first scene, she made herself up on film to be a white-haired scientist, searching the shape of the galaxy. In the second, there was a nude scene of her lightly masturbating with the side of a model Saturn launcher, the third scene she made up to be an actress languorously and writhingly pouring over her text. Lastly, he told her to stand in the doorway looking at the cover of *The Theater of Cruelty* intently, and to fall straight backward after one minute. She was frightened for the first time and protested that she would hurt herself. Trust me, he said, I'll be kneeling behind you and catch you before you hit the floor. His cameraman and light and sound techs looked on silently until she decided yes.

She worked herself into a state of total shock, visualizing her mother having discovered her with Moisheh and the two kids on sleeping pills, and fell straight back. Her head smashed the floor.

"Perfect, perfect," he was yelling excitedly. "That was great." The other three men looked at her afraid to move. She hurt, she hated him. She'd been totally had. But she would never admit it. This hate, cold, severe, profound would be her acting secret. She knew she had discovered her force.

She told her mother the film had never been finished but she showed her the two thousand and took her mother out to the Russian tearoom. She graduated at seventeen and took a job in a drama movie bookstore in Midtown.

One day a guy strode in and bought some Brecht, Stanislavsky, Albee, and Beckett. "What do you know that's past the Theater of Cruelty," she dared him with her greenest gaze. That stopped him not at all. "The Theater of Infinite Montage," he grinned. "Who did that?" She asked.

"No one, I'm doing it now. "

"Need another actress?"

For the next seven years they worked together. He showed her breathing, movement, gestures, quick changes, voice, emotions, everything but characters. She thought she could use all these nearly magical techniques to develop the ability to play characters, to become a star. Harry had studied all over the planet, he could do almost anything except write a play with living characters that would pack them in. Harry didn't even want to pack them in. His ambition was to travel Europe and the USA with his small troupe and he never minded rolling the bus into the woods or even a tall cornfield and pulling out the sleeping bags. Harry's motto was Perform and Split. He never played anywhere more than a week. In the summers he'd never go to the festivals where they paid good. They spent the summers preparing the next season in a big barn in Florida. Hot.

Of course she had also gotten involved with Harry. They had two things in common, a driving hunger to master the tricks of theater, of the human body and its emotions and desires and dreams, and a hot sex connection. But Harry never wanted fame, and she did, and Harry never wanted her alone, and she either wanted that or total freedom. She bided her time. When she turned twenty-four, she saw Harry for what he was, a man so interested in his idea, even his insight, that humans were super clever montaging units, multi-phrenics, rags on a tall pole he called super objectives, which themselves changed with every twist of history, personal, social or cosmic, that he had forgotten all about getting it across to the people, to become, and rightly so, famous. Harry loved putting on a play in Paris for five nights to elite audiences of fifty or sixty a night and then talking to the members of the audience for two hours after the play when she wanted to go out in the town and relax.

She found a New Age tough guru attending one set of Harry's performances. One of his young broad-shouldered black-haired young men fell for her big. Harry never even noticed. Harry was convinced she was as nuts for what he called pure theater as he was. He was also convinced Art plus good Sex always outweighed great Sex.

She came back late to rehearsal one evening and kissed the young man goodbye full in the mouth at the back of the theater. "That's an odd way to say good-bye," said Harry. "Oh, that's how everybody does it who's in the movies," she said. Harry laughed. He believed it she saw because he thought the movies weren't the real thing. Image is a thin soup of the Body and the Body is the proper field of art. Since the movies were phony to him on first principles, Harry found nothing unusual in the idea of phony kisses. Maud felt suddenly her hatred rise again like a knife. Harry had taken her for a fall harder and longer than Hiromoto. This guy could perform miracles with his voices, resonating chambers, and weird attention exercises, but he didn't know from nothing about real life anymore than Hiromoto did.

In Paris just after this she fell to talking with genuine interest for the first time to a member of the audience. She ordinarily sat uncomfortable and scornful of all talk other than artistic. This lady was beautiful, graceful, vivacious at fifty. Maud went out with her to her luxurious apartment above the Quai Voltaire where a slim Gabonese servant made them comfortable. The lady revealed to Maud the secret of her long-lasting beauty and it had to do with sexual fulfillment. She had character, she understood life, she was a mistress of life.

Maud left early in the morning and ran up the river to the crash pad where the theater members had fallen asleep. After packing her things she bent over Harry and poured a Coca Cola over his face. She watched him struggle to do one of his favorite exercises, dealing with given circumstances.

In the past she would have admired his supercool. Now she only saw his repertoire.

"I'm leaving. Don't you dare try to find me."

She tried out at the great Peter Brooks Theater. She tried out on Broadway. She went to Hollywood. She was never broke because she used her sex wisely and well. She got a contact with Columbia. No big role ever came. No role came for a year. Her chin was a little too long. Her hair was not quite that abundant. Though that could be helped it could not be solved.

After three years she got her name in the titles as number five in a medium budget movie as a querulous Jewish nurse. That was it.

She could not figure who she hated worse, Hiromoto or Harry or life itself.

She fell ill and became thin, even gaunt.

Harry's theater became broke and busted in Brazil earning his first national headlines. She called the TV people and got paid five thousand dollars to tell thirteen per cent of the American viewing public how right the Brazilians were to have seen through those frauds who sacrificed themselves and victims like herself at the altar of some insane idea of perfection in art. "They worship beauty in a world full of poverty and ugliness," she cried into the mike, "It is an obscene cult ignoring reality. They deserve a Brazilian jail."

She felt a glow of happiness. Her appearance had been a smash. She had reached the public. She had proved she could handle it. Had proved it above all to Harry. Now it all made sense to her, why jealous people had held her down. What a shame she'd fallen terminally ill. Now only she would really know what the world had missed.

The Chemist Who Got It All Figured Out

December, 1976

Max Warneke stood tall and lean, green eyes flaming above a prominent curved nose with wide nostrils, a shock of black hair brushed mercilessly back with a hundred strokes each morning. He made his money as a chemist at Western Mine Mills and Smelters' new uranium crushing and leaching plant in Navajo country. Max preferred the Pueblo Indians and their Apollonian correctness in following the settled rituals of a successful thousand year life in which, without ever specializing in fighting, they had survived Navajo, Spanish, and American attacks. They had their big moments like when they made rain storms come by intensely concentrated dances and drumming, or by their rattle snake dance, or by drifting down the cold dawn slopes of the Jemez incarnating deer, or striding through Zuni as a giant god surrounded by severely irreverent mudheads who pissed on all pomposities.

Max spoke of all these matters with the studied precision of Bridgemanian and Popperian scientific lingo, as a pure succession of operations that so far produced the predicted result, and as hypotheses that could be falsified by such a non-recurrence. Nonetheless, he had become a self-educated specialist on rain events, and a friend to several of the medicine men who ran the secret societies in the kiva that produced them.

At the age of twenty-five, in 1962, he felt that he had become "someone". He felt this so strongly, purely, that he never felt the need for recognition. Someone "who could really do it" could remain unknown, untargeted, free to move like the wind, unaccountable to the institutions that seemed to him empty of truth, no matter what power they exercised. He was a good, even brilliant, analytical chemist. His standards were higher than the company's so he had no problems filling his job. Devoid of any managerial ambition, so devoid he did not even have to be flattered by the manager, he threatened no one. He had calculated the job, or its equivalent elsewhere, was his for life. A one-time exchange with society that paid enough to settle all his obligations, securing all his material needs, locating him in country (the Four Corners) that he belonged to, though born in Connecticut's tree-filled land which bored him with its small vistas. His job kept him up with technical progress which was his complementary admiration besides the Pueblo traditions. He liked mining's time after time devouring all of its old production forms and methods and recreating them in newer, more exact, higher tonnage systems.

He had discovered a smooth-skinned young rancher's girl on a Saturday night dance and his sexual life was properly released every weekend. He planned on no marriage, having had all the domestic stupidity he needed for the rest of his life from observing his paunchy father and mushy mother going at it with their unaesthetic seriousness.

One day, one of his Pueblo learned men took him to a peyote lodge. He heard amazing drumming, heard true speech, smelled the cedar, watched the fire, flickering with its every flicker, had gone out to vomit once. But he had no vision as it was clear so many had. He had slipped into no deep trance, communing with an inner-self. His sensations had all become extraordinarily acute far beyond his already remarked keen eyesight and his ability to smell a new chemical in the lab before anyone else. He believed he could smell hydrogen, officially "odorless", and had run several tests that gave him, he thought, ninety percent certainty that, in fact, he could detect it by nose alone. But never had he heard such sighs, drumbeats, rhythmic changes, seen each spark and flicker, touched earth's and wool's textures so minutely.

At last he had found his own chemical project. How to ingest peyote without vomiting or wishing to, and what amount would be required to gain him a vision, or to prove to him conclusively, ex operation, ex hypothesis, that there was no vision in him to gain and that regardless of whether the Indians had really only pretended to vision out of the stores of their cultural poetry being brought to a creative point by the circle of their palpable expectation, to find out about the truth of his own capacity.

The first step proved surprisingly easy. Add a base such as Coca Cola to peyote juice extracted from the plant and the taste was bearable. The second step had been to study the botany and ecology of the plant and then go on a collecting trip, to fill a basket with one hundred "buttons". The third step was to set up a security procedure, since peyote, while legal for Indians, was not for whites or blacks, a peculiar travesty of racism he thought, since physiological differences were so small.

His weekends became decidedly more interesting. The increase in his sensations occurred also sexually. He did not give Eileen any of this juice and allayed any possible eighteen year old curiosity by stating he had some wine with a friend at Western before coming over. Up to eight buttons, he had no visions, whereupon he stopped since the acuteness of sensation fell off for him, but due to a sort of dullness rather than the onset of a trance or contemplative state such as he had read about. He got closer to that state when he was catwalking on the edge of a dangerous overhang with Eileen crying out to him to be careful every time he took a careful, calculated risk.

One Saturday afternoon after ingesting, he went into a pool hall; his shots were as on as before, only the pink five ball turned especially vividly pink and he did think that never had he seen pink before.

Some Chicano kids that had started visiting him in his small two-room adobe outside of Grants brought him some marijuana one Sunday evening. They took him in their old pick-up out on a big ranch where it grew in a back canyon. He ought to see the cows groove on this, they laughed. They moo like they're playing jazz. The marijuana relaxed him, but he saw nothing he had not already sensed on full moonlit nights when the boys said they saw scenes he wouldn't believe going on in the shadows beneath the cottonwoods.

Some years later, visiting his parents in Connecticut, listening to them tell him he would inherit none of their property unless he got married, he split into Manhattan in his jeans, buckskin shirt, and moccasins to cruise on a hot July night in a place he'd heard a lot about, Washington Square. He had his eyes open and soon had a dark slim girl listening to his yarns about the old Southwest and the ways of its Indians.

They had almost immediately vibed their longings into synch as they strolled around the park without holding hands. Finally, she invited him to her apartment on East 62nd, complete with door guard. The old noisy elevator had been torn down for these professional new people to live in a sanitized Baghdad-on-the-Hudson.

He expected her to suggest playing a record, some wine, a look from the balcony, etcetera, but she invited him to try mescaline, the potent compound in peyote. Mescaline seemed to his bodily taste to be a union of the finest wine and the purest peyote ceremony. She suggested nothing else, but the rest of the evening unfolded new insights to him on how to live and love, using the space of her Persian carpet. He didn't have a vision, but he almost did. He could say "This is not a Persian carpet, it's a magic carpet." But it remained a metaphor and not a vision. She was lithe, responsive, manifesting, but she remained a girl, although the loveliest he had ever seen, and never became a vision. He noted the freckles on her neck, the mole on her chin, the slightly sharp elbows, and all of the almost perfect points.

The next day, he said to himself, mescaline has got to be the champagne of these compounds. He studied for a week, then after experimenting in his red lab beneath his mother's kitchen, he perfected making it, testing each purification with Sarah, his new sidekick. "The old Priest and Puritans are cracking down on everything now that might enhance a person's sensations, health and emotions, that may even give some a true vision, though I haven't had any. From what you told me you paid for that sample, you and I could make a million in about two years, split it, and be free for the rest of our lives. Doing well by doing good. This compound will only be popular among the most discriminating and most successful. I make it and you flog it."

She made a long scene with him. They'd never be able to stop before it was too late. Mescaline was not addictive or dangerous, it was a wonderful discovery, but money was addictive, dangerous, a discovery that had nearly wrecked the very Indian cultures he so loved. They should keep living as they had been, simply, freely.

He informed her he was a man without vision; he sensed and he thought. He would like to have more emotions, but he feared negative emotions more than he desired positive emotions so he kept himself in perfect physical and intellectual condition, stropped to the razor's edge. She need have no fear about his getting carried away by anything.

By 1970 they had made their million. He destroyed all his laboratory equipment, all his supplies, all his product. He told her they were splitting. She said why, it had all been so perfect. He said, one day you may threaten me, I don't want you even to have that temptation. You'll miss your mescaline as well as me, she cried out in many complex locutions, but he only laughed.

"I have the perfect consolation," he said in considerably less ornamented language. "Money for life, freedom to travel and live where I wish. And I did finally get my vision. Be a man who figured it all out and won as much as can be won from life's crooked game and then split the house before it took revenge on his copping their scene."

The Director Who Became
a Guru

June, 1983

Immanuel was born on Second Avenue near Sixth Street in
Manhattan. The family didn't have much money, but they always
ate out twice a week at a Ukrainian restaurant, a low cost hang out
for Slavs and broke Bohemian artists, from the time Immanuel
could remember, when he was about four. Immanuel Kolkhanov
had the broad half-Tatar face of a Russian peasant Tolstoy would
have sat down to talk to, but his eyes flamed with a brown virtuosity
that could have come only from a Jewish mother.

From his father he got supple movement and athletic
prowess; from his mother the seeing of emotional weaknesses of
others, plus a good defense, a permanent emotional attack mode. He
never claimed to be good at mathematics or philosophy. His senior
year at high school he became an expert fencer and spent all the
time he could in the theater and going to new Off-Off Broadway
productions.

He got into CCNY and made an immediate hit with his
blonde teacher from Radcliffe, who was looking for the "talent she
knew was buried there" in the non-Anglo-Saxons. She tagged
Immanuel and a moody rhetorical black girl as the ones to whom
she would "transmit real drama."

Immanuel soon adopted a *nom de guerre* in order to win
the success war, "Fred Adkins." Six years later, at the age of
twenty-four, he pulled ten of his former classmates and two Off-
Broadway actors together to do a Sean O'Casey production. He got

it backed through an angel the Cliffie Prof introduced him to. Not a smash, it did run for three months, with reviews in the Times, the Post and the Voice. "A cast magically welded together in its movements and gestures, revealing the emotional planes of weakness and nostalgia like mirrors," was his favorite quote.

He then met Count Mumford, an exponent of his own synthesis of Gurdieff, Meyerhold, and Krishnamurti. "Super-effort in a group! Biomechanics for your body! You're on your own emotionally!" Count Mumford was extremely attractive to ladies of a certain age and older, and to men of a certain social class, although two or three he didn't charge when their assets dwindled in return for contributing managerial services on his Rye estate. "People interested in these kind of ideas always have a certain weakness for titles," he would comment in a charmingly modest self-deprecatory tone when asked how he attracted his circle of some two hundred. The Count himself, however, who worked part-time in a New York financial firm, "to keep a balance between the inner and the outer man", sometimes wished "to see what new forces the collective unconscious is spewing forth". So on a warm July evening, one of his down-at-the-heels gentlemen, who specialized in what to do in the evenings, took the Count, by his own request, to see Fred Adkins' biomechanics and Reichian catharses efficiently twisting the bodies of twelve actors through all the phases of nostalgic purple ruins of Irish dust. An additional interest in the play to the Count, was that he had always held that it was not the Boer War but the refusal to grant Home Rule to Ireland that provoked German hopes to overthrow the Empire.

The Count, quite taken by the complex movements and emotional precision of the work, asked Stanley, his gentleman Virgil, to take him over to meet Adkins. "With emotions and movements but little intellect, he's only got two out of three centers going. But, that's twice as many as the ordinary man. Let's see if he wants to learn to count to three and get some ideas as well."

The tall, rangy, gray-haired Count, gray-eyed, in tweed sport coat, and the five-foot ten-inch stocky young East Side black-haired man in T-shirt and jeans, shook hands, each confronting the other, each easily using the techniques that had made them such influences on other human beings. They both gently made it clear that they were sizing each other up before speaking. They both took it as a compliment.

"Should we talk?" asked the Count in a negligent tone.

"Yes," said Adkins, who had been told a bit about the Count by Stanley who had gotten free tickets arranged more as a recognition of the Count than to save money, though Stanley had personally fallen to the point of counting his ten spots. Adkins insisted on taking them to a hip new steak house on Thompson Street, the colors being black and white, tall mirrors and brown wooden tables and chairs.

"A man like you," said the Count, "attains early the power to enchant and lead a few people in his chosen profession, simply by the skilled expression of his powerful physical emotional temperament. However," (and the Count almost hissed, as his face subtly became snakelike in its strike) "you are nothing but meat. Immortality is the only aim for a Real Man."

Adkins could not and did not even try to prevent his sitting bolt upright. For the first time in his new life, since becoming Adkins instead of Kolkhanov, Adkins met a man who knew more than he did, who had access to some exact knowledge that he needed. Whether or not in the end he would use it to try to gain immortality or choose to develop new powers to play the better with life while it lasted. He looked at Stanley, but the Count with an elegant wave of his right hand indicated Stanley was an okay part of the scene. "Tell me more," said Adkins. "I'm ready to learn." Adkins knew instinctively that demonstrating the promise to be a top student was the supreme flattery one could offer to a man setting himself to teach. Minimum, he wanted to acquire the Count's grand and easy manner, that was for sure.

Adkins had three more personal meetings with the Count, then attended two of his advanced classes in music and movement, saw how he could take these ideas and methods, adopt them to his director's know-how and produce a drama in the midst of life that would attract all the types of people he wanted to experiment with and find out about. The Count became concerned about Adkins' attitude and its effect on the sexual emotional tenor of the well-organized life on his estate. They parted on friendly terms, agreeing to stay in touch, the Count anticipating subtle pleasures in watching a sorcerer's apprentice drown himself in the flood he would raise, and Adkins congratulating himself on having gained a prestigious reference point, "My teacher was Count Mumford."

Adkins confronted his actors with his break-through approach. Did they wish to become Real Men and Real Women, masters of their own destiny, he demanded, or stay actors dependent on the vagaries of a stupid commercial world gaining such fame, love and thrills as luck might throw their way, till old age and death disposed of their pretensions. As for him, his life had been transformed by deciding to be a Real Man and finding the teaching that had shown him how. He let his eyes pierce them, just ten percent off from a full hypnotic glare. He then did a perfect imitation of the Count's negligent, don't care what you do myself, patrician tone.

They all signed on, impressed by Fred's accession of a commanding confidence, and by his assertion that the teaching he had found would work a profound change in their lives as it had clearly changed him. Fred arranged a trip to Belize. He gave out his first "essence task." "Get the money to do this and in one month."

He went up one afternoon to Count Mumford's estate to see Marion, a spectacular blonde, who read books and was the companion of Dexter who played the philosopher role to

Mumford's king. He saw her and made straight towards her. "Marion," he said, "you are a red-blooded passionate brilliant woman. Come with me, I'm starting a fast action group. You don't need to waste your time with any more philosophic bullshit. I need you to help me. You've studied this stuff for years. You know it and I can do it. Together we'll make a real school. You know Dexter's just going to spend the next forty years philosophizing. He's a nice guy. He needs you. But you need me. And I can make good use of your knowledge."

He rented a large bungalow remote in the Mayan mountains. They could hear jaguars in the night and howler monkeys in the early mornings. "All of you wear false masks, you've hidden your real face, you have no idea what your real desires are, what your real type-limitations are. Now you are going to find out." They stayed up all night every other night and took night walks in the jungle, terrifying, since none of them had ever been in tropical wilderness. They changed partners, except Fred and Marion. They were thrown into scenes to express each emotion that rose within. In two weeks, four had left Fred, two disgusted, one desperate and the fourth obsessively counting his fucks. But the remaining eight had become followers. Fred had manifested unbroken confidence, and deepened his sex-mind relation with Marion, as well as his top position as director of the scenes and critic of the players.

Back in the Village, he took a loft and charged eighty dollars a month per person. He put one man and one woman in charge of recruiting. He made a theater, a being confrontation room for his talks where he singled out individuals for confrontations on their weaknesses, and a kitchen, so they could have a weekly dinner together. He set up special exercises so that the members would increase their power to set an internal aim and achieve it. He began to believe he was who he said he was, an advanced man, a Real Man, who had made an immortal body inside his mortal body, and who could show other less gifted people how to achieve this also but of course in a longer time. Marion kept getting him books to read that she remembered from the Count's library. He ransacked them for exercises he could assign. He found his students, as he now called them, were mad for exercises. Each exercise would give a new spirit, a new insight, made them feel they were going somewhere, made him feel he was a real teacher. Marion then fed him several new exercises, each of which she had promised the Count to keep secret. Each new exercise he got made him a bolder lover. She loved this power she had to increase his power. The group grew to thirty and he moved to a somewhat grand apartment but with little furniture. He took on a statuesque black maid. Marion became pregnant, and caught him with the maid. "You're a talk machine," he shouted. "I need a passion machine. Talk is boring."

"It wasn't boring for two years."

"Yeah, but I learned all you knew, all you have to say, now it bores me. Sex is creative energy, it's always new."

They broke up, but he supported her in another apartment. No new students were allowed to meet her, but the old ones could. He was crazy over the baby boy. He stayed there every Saturday night.

A girl went bananas in one of his break-down-the-mask attacks. She lost her acting job, her boyfriend, she killed herself.

He dropped out of the theater crowd. People stared at him when he had tried to keep showing himself at theater events. The story of the girl was known by many. Her younger sister, also in theater, in costumes, had become his enemy. He went to the Count who received him with four attendants. "I can have nothing more to do with you, Fred. You tried to go too far, too soon, on too little. I am not a sorcerer, I am a master player in the master game, but you took it as sorcery, as a quick way to obtain dangerous powers. You have no sense of humor." The old Count smiled. "Only total humiliation could save you now, Fred, and then only if you took it right. You would have to beg each person you claimed to teach for forgiveness."

Fred broke off from the Count. He decided to become an outlaw until he could make new law that would beat all the old laws about self-transformation.

He heard about Haight-Ashbury. He dropped his whole New York group. "Good-bye," he said. "You're on your own now, I need better material. You've gone as far as you can go. You started too late in life." He dropped his new wife too, a tall dark Jewish singer who had tried to "save him."

He had an introduction to a girl, Elaine. Coming by to see her in North Beach, he found her and a houseful of people, twenty in all, between eighteen and twenty-three years old, headed for redwoods for the weekend. Elaine invited him to join. "I've heard about you, too" she said, "that you have some powers."

That weekend, curious, he unleashed a full set of exercises on this excited, idealistic crowd all high on hashish. The results convinced him he was indeed a Real Man. They all wanted more. Elaine climbed into his bed.

He had found his milieu. "Ecstasy is man's natural state," he would orate. "No Real Man needs a drug and a Real Woman needs a Real Man. Sex is a hang up, find the type you really go for. Experiment. Money is a hang up. Go out and get it. We're going to buy two hundred acres and live the essence of life. Power is a hang up. Go confront people. Rise above the hassle getting you. Get what your aim is even if it's only to stand an inch taller in front of some type that used to make you squirm, act deferential, like a shit-head or a cunt." He started using four letter words in great profusion. He'd seen Peter O'Toole do this once in a theater rehearsal to dominate the scene.

Before long, he had two hundred students at two hundred dollars a month. He bought a mansion for Marion to join him and had another child. He tried to go back into theater. He wrote plays based on medieval morality plays. His students flogged tickets. It failed. Then he found his oracle, a woman who gave him answers, not exercises. He found hard-boiled young men, who wanted to be in a dominating group and "live like Fred', a Real Man.

"I don't worry about failing in the theater," he told them, "the public's not ready for real ideas and it builds my being."

"My teaching is strictly how to gain immortality."

He had to leave California. He tried Alaska, Oregon, New York again, and settled down in a remote farm in New England with his oracle. A core of his students stayed loyal to him. "Those were real experiences, weren't they," he would ask.

"They certainly were. And we're passing them on."

He hadn't done at all badly, he thought, for a half-breed boy from the Lower East Side. And who really knew? He had buried something inside. No one knew he had a broken heart. That was being, wasn't it, to continue confidently with a broken heart. That was Stanislavsky's magic carried to the last note of the octave. If anybody in his generation had built an alchemical body to survive death, it could just as well be him. And if Monty Python was right that it was all a pile of shit, at least his turds were more interesting, or at least as interesting as anybody else's when it came to final count-down. As long as he didn't commit suicide, nobody'd ever find out. He'd fooled them all and got by with it. If he kept doing it until he died it'd even be authentic, it would be his own chosen existence, his own way he'd intentionally played life's card. Perhaps he would even become real. After all a human could never tell.

The Orator Ruined
by Philosophy

March, 1982

B ill Martin's mother and father died when he was two years old,
at the age of thirty-eight and fifty respectively. They left an
estate just large enough for his aunt, his father's sister, to come back
from Europe and raise him from the age of four in east Texas in the
old two-story frame house, sweet-smelling from its extensive
honeysuckles in the shade of the century-old live oaks that
surrounded it and made its adjacent vacant corner lot into a small
woodland. His father also left him an album devoted to his
grandfather, a statuesque slave owner and general in the
Confederate Army.

His slim aristocratic aunt, was forty-ish and a spinster, but
she had earned a small living assisting curators in provincial
museums in Italy and France. During the war she had worked in
Boston at the Fogg. She believed that the early deaths of Will
Rogers, Thomas Wolfe and F. Scott Fitzgerald had ruined the
chances of American culture. They were the ones destined to make
sense out of World War II and bring America into self-
understanding via humor, poignancy and tragedy respectively. Now
perhaps no sense would ever be made of America. That had
happened with some cultures like the Hondurans and the
Rumanians. Nonetheless Bill could become civilized and travel.

She looked upon the chance to raise Bill Martin as her
chance to transmit her cultural learning to a vital brilliant American
child. Lord knew that America needed every conscious individual it
could get to keep the savor in its salt. Bill's father had been a

hulking figure of an east Texas hunter, fisherman and politician. Bill inherited the physique and vitality from him and now he would develop the brains from her, his father's sister.

He began to take elocution at nine years old from a Presbyterian organist, a simple big-bosomed woman who smelled of camellias and taught him the artifices of the rise and fall of the voice. His aunt, Tante, he called her, made sure he did his homework and had a library of art reproductions and history books appropriate to his interests. She encouraged his high school friendship with the other two brightest boys in his class and for him to take speech, act in plays and enter the national debate contest.

He could not get the hang of dating girls. Who was he to face rejection from one of those creatures? He became afraid of his intense intellectual admiration for his two friends, one, Jack, a daredevil inventor and car racer, destined everyone said to die young breaking his neck or become a millionaire, and two, Richard, who already wore glasses at fifteen, but could play tennis well enough to avoid the sissy label, and who prosaically but thoroughly debated Bill on any and every point at the drop of a hat. Bill discovered the fusion of imagination and masturbation and decided this would solve the problem of his sex energy until he found the right girl at college. He liked the taste of whisky, but could take it or leave it. He won the national debating contest and became a momentary local celebrity, "that boy with a great future." Heads would nod towards him.

Tante was proud and confident of him when he left Sandy Creek for the State University. He had been valedictorian, Richard had been the salutatorian and Jack the outstanding senior. Tante loved to make them a French dinner each week and listen to their talk. She knew something was lacking in them, something no European, at least continental European, grew up without and this worried her deeply gazing on their excited good looking American faces and thick shocks of hair. They had no sense of ambiguity, little irony and as to the shadow side of life, they supposed that to be lying in the cool shade of the live oaks on a hot cricket-mad August afternoon.

At the University Bill met Professor Heinrich Kohl. Heinrich Kohl had left Germany not when Hitler came to power, but ten years before when he had thought Germany would go Bolshevik from the inflation sufferings. Kohl could not forget seeing pianos being thrown out of second story windows in Munich in the communists' fight against the Republic. He was sixty when Bill met him in his first class in philosophy as a sophomore.

History, he said to Bill, is not the development of any continuity such as progress but rather a succession of eruptions of phenomena in each of which, if it is a great epoch, a philosopher arises to elucidate its central idea while that idea or truth is cast into a form or beauty by great artists who render the experience of their epoch available to any who can fathom that artist. For example, Heraclitus and Homer, Bacon and Shakespeare, Kant and Goethe, Nietszche and Dostoyevsky. He invited Bill to play chess with him once a week in the arbor behind his modest professor's cottage. "Neither a cynic's barrel, nor an epicurean estate," he said. "Nor a stoic's frontier nor a sceptic's salon," Bill replied.

Bill became the students' main speaker on the civil rights issues, to break the segregation on campus at the graduate student level. He and Richard set up a lunch table in the old restaurant above the cottage bookstore. The leaders of all the campus organizations came to the weekly meeting. They planned monthly demonstrations that led to Bill's set piece speeches. "Education is for the mind, not the skin. Education cannot flower half-free and half-ghettoed."

His finest hour. No National Guard or U.S. Marshalls were needed to break the graduate school segregation. To be sure, this small victory in 1950, intense as had been its battles, had only scratched the skin of America's tragedy. What would he do next?

Why did he not become a philosopher, Heinrich suggested, puffing from his textured pipe carved in Switzerland. Bill also puffed from his plain briar pipe. What is truth, he said he wanted to know, yes, but in his heart he felt there was no truth. He could look below the surface, sometimes just right at the surface, anywhere in Texas and see that.

He discussed fluently in his senior year all the core issues with Heinrich, the flux of Heraclitus, the unchanging world of Parmenides, the duty of Marcus Aurelius, the garden of small real pleasures of Epicurus, the intellectual love of God or nature of Spinoza, the absolute God of total determination of Newton, the death of God of Nietszche, the idealistic dialectic of Hegel, the materialist dialectic of Marx ("A dog pissing on the front of the cathedral of Hegel," said Heinrich), the truth is what works of Dewey, the variety of experiences of James, the equivalence of logic and mathematics of Russell, the Homeric world of the immediate and vivid, Voltairian mockery of hypocrisy, Kant's critique of pure sterile reason, but what was his own philosophy? He had no clue. If not a philosopher, why not a Cicero, why had he not continued with his oratory, his speaking, his life in the nation with his fellow citizens?

He knew the answer. He could not talk with anyone about the truth of his own life. He had found his sexual milieu hanging out as a graduate student through the Korean war. He had a hidden leather jacket. He liked being beaten and sometimes he liked to beat. He had found a secret group. He could see all the playacting around him. Richard would become a professor and look at all sides (all legal sides) of a question in politics with his fine smile implying an "enlightened educated public" would "make a real difference". That's it, nothing would disturb Richard's life, ever, until it came time to die and then he would take intelligent doses of morphine. Richard was already looking for a good liberal wife, even thinking of a certain colorful Jewish girl from a Manhattan intelligentsia family, though he had found out that they used to belong to the Party (but not after the Czechoslovakian takeover). Jack was making out with the cheerleader and sorority crowd. He had already made ten grand his junior summer with an annealing invention he had helped make in a Detroit foundry.

It was not just Bill's sex life, though he could be thrown in jail for that if discovered, certainly it would be difficult to teach philosophy without being fired. But it was not just possible punishments. He looked around and found nothing behind all the playacting. He had read his Henry James by now. He would have been happy to go European, to acknowledge evil and sorrow as permanent leitmotifs, to have become as ambiguous and ironic as Heinrich in some tolerable state university.

But he could not see or even sniff any evil. He only saw stupidity, stuffed people stuffing their faces, thinking as little as possible, blurred in their sensations, almost dead in their emotions. Even the atomic bomb was simply calculated as a game and if they were ever unleashed, it would be by a mathematical mistake, not from any real position. No one would be standing behind it. The world had destroyed Hitler and would forget Stalin. Good, but who had won? The American middle class? The world middle class? What did Bill Martin, grandson of a Southern aristocrat have to do with the middle class and its money grabbing, thing acquiring, idea fearing, artist despising, church pewed moral mediocrity. Nothing! he answered himself. I have nothing to do with these pigs and prigs.

Heinrich on the strength of Bill's Master's thesis on Existentialism and the Theater of the Absurd, which won a national prize, got him into a doctoral program at a University in Los Angeles. Bill finished his coursework with A's, but never found a mentor like Heinrich. One of the professors, the idealist, had invited him to tea with his wife, another to Sunday sherry with his fanatic devotees to logical positivism, but it was clear to all that only Bill's manners saved the events from total disaster. His manners could not conceal his contempt for philosophy turned into a cushy job purveying specialist logical acrobatics. "Where is the love of Wisdom?" he had permitted himself to say at the logical positivist's stucco house in West Hollywood.

At thirty, he was abruptly thrown out for not completing his dissertation on the Meaning of Meaninglessness. He alternated between high cool beat sessions with Larry Lipton and acolytes in early morning hours, and being a car wash attendant. He found a lady, Jean, a sociologist who made a living working for the county, who believed in "his genius". She gave him a bed in a small room off the porch of her cottage. Doing her day's work with the desperate, and uneducated, going by the book as she had to do, and dealing with the crises of her growing child, left her hair damp, her face sallow, fattened her body, left her without any vigor to spark the sexual flow. There was little meat in her diet except an occasional fish. She would listen to Bill talk for an hour about ideas after dinner. It kept her life cultured. It paid his room and board. She replaced his aunt with her care for him and demanded much less from his brain in return.

Richard stopped welcoming him to visit at his oak-pathed, Ivy League school "until you become productive" and perform minimal duties of citizenship. "Well, yes, like voting, if you want to be direct about it." Jack still welcomed him once a week in his Beverly Hills house filled with the perfect billiards room for Jack "to concentrate on the laws of mechanics, the only perfect achievement of the human intellect, that exposes the fraudulent pretensions of all the philosophers."

Bill did not consider himself unhappy. He smoked his briar pipe with devotion. He had passionate scenes that, he thought, were better than de Sade's because his were for real, and he stayed out of prison. He had an almost carefree liberal bohemian home life with a fridge full of good things, a good wine, the New York Times, excellent records, and curious discussions on Jean's specialty, culturology. He read intensely and wildly. The Possessed he contrasted with The Magic Bead Game. War and Peace he worked out step by step against The Red and Black. The Tropics of Capricorn and Cancer against Tender is the Night. Huckleberry Finn against The Sun Also Rises. Michelangelo against Leonardo. Rubens against Modigliani. Burroughs against de Quincey. De Sade against Jane Austen.

"Don't you feel you are wasting your genius, your epoch, your friends' time?" Jean asked him.

"No," he said. "I feel I'm living my brief life the best way I know how to. A philosopher is not wise, that's a sage, a philosopher loves wisdom, which implies wisdom is other than he. Call me what you will, you could be right, I know only what I love and that's all I will sacrifice my life to. Screw the rest of it!" He laughed for once so ferociously that she left the room, guessing the awful truth. She cried bitterly.

Jack Moore

November, 1970

Jack Moore had it made in the shade that yellow leafed October of Nineteen Fifty-Nine in Ohio. He taught sculpture half-time at the University with access to its superb furnaces and studio space. The governor had bought his Berkshire Pig sculpture, a magnificent swine rooting for something precious in the dirt. His pieces were in demand by the well-off businessmen and by the museums in the state. He had won a couple of national ribbons. His wife, a thin black-haired woman adored his talent and believed his name would last in the annals of art. His boy at the age of nine was a genial rascal and Jack had just sculpted him as Huck Finn gazing, presumably at the Mississippi, certainly at some sight provoking a boy's leisured spacing out.

His wife, Betty, wanted to be a writer above all else, uncover the secret motives that abruptly changed human lives. She had just introduced Jack to a young tall writer, shy and incandescent by turns, who had visited her writers' workshop. "You have got to talk to each other," she said, blithely eager for abrupt change in her own life. The young man, Marley Peterson, and Jack looked at each other for a minute of rising recognition. She left, knowing she had changed everything.

"Seeing you completes my decision," said Jack and grabbed hold of a wonderfully real whiteface bull. "I'm going to smash every piece in my shop and head for New York. This place is killing me!"

"You can't do that," Marley protested. "It's beautiful."

"It's beautiful. It's beautiful," Jack mocked him. "I thought Betty said you were a genius poet, with touches of Catullus and Blake. I don't believe her now. Where do you see any Catullus in this bull destined to sit on the fireplace of some cattle breeder running for Senator?"

Marley shrugged under the intensity. Sure, there was no Catullus in the bull. "But it's valuable, sell it to pay your way to New York. You'll need the money".

"What I need is myself," snarled Jack. He dashed the bull on the concrete floor of his garage studio. In a methodic rage, he took down each of the pieces on his shelves and smashed them to shards.

"That one," cried Marley, "that one has some Catullus," he pointed to a flat chested woman with a gaping vagina, thin shoulders hunched in pain, about to give birth. "Take it then," Jack grinned. "You are the first patron of my new era. I'm going to start all over again, die in the attempt or become a real sculptor, expressing something of what I see, clichés of the local herd."

"Why is her chest so flat?"

"Because my wife's chest is flat and she's the only woman I've ever touched and so that's all of woman I know as a sculptor."

Jack and Marley became friends. Marley wanted to go to New York too, but he had hitchhiked and freight-trained around the West and Midwest, with a notebook, Ezra Pound, Catullus and Rimbaud tucked in his army jacket.

Jack left Betty two days later and drove Marley to Pittsburgh where Marley wanted to experience the steel industry and rivers, their stench, noise, flaming dust, opulent bars and "Little Chicago" mobs. On the way, the right front tire blew out and Jack barely held the old Dodge on the highway.

"Close," said Marley.

"If I die, I don't care if it's with you," replied Jack.

Marley was not attracted physically, but he felt that emotionally he was now bound to Jack in some passionate way.

Jack wrote him a couple of letters from New York. In the mid–sixties, Marley hitch-hiked there and was left off at Seventh and West Fourth after coming through the Hudson tunnel from the marshes of Jersey.

He pressed a buzzer on Perry Street. The shady trees, the brownstones, the frank glances of the girls made him feel as if he were already a citizen of the Village.

Jack waved him in. Over a coffee in dim light, Jack told Marley his story. He had arrived in New York with fifty dollars, the winter coming on, no clothes except what he wore, an overcoat, hat, sweater, an extra pair of socks, thick shoes.

Jack felt he had to die to be reborn. How to do that? He had no time for esoteric bullshit. He decided to act as if he were dead. He walked down sidewalks and across streets without looking. Nobody punched him or ran over him. After two weeks he'd begun to come to life. Why take up with women if he didn't want another child. They took tremendous emotional effort. Sex was necessary only to keep physical chemical balance.

Nightly, he had done the meatwalk past all the guys on Christopher Street. When he was living again and sexually balanced, he found one guy, a musician, who leased this pad, and they got along well together. Played a weekly game of chess, enjoyed a weekly dinner out with a good wine. Both liked a clean apartment with no luxury to distract them from their work. He had joint use of a furnace and studio with another sculptor three blocks away on Hudson.

"Here, look at these two pieces," Jack said laying aside a covering canvas and showing them to Marley. "I'm having a show next month on Madison Street." Jack smiled confidently.

Marley looked at them quite some time. Perhaps he didn't see something in the hammered lead surfaces, almost two dimensional, representing graceful abstractions of two human figures. Jack's lips curled partly in anger, partly in sorrow, partly in malice. "You don't see any Catullus, huh? Well, he was no sculptor. But you probably don't see any Cellini either. Hell, it's lead, not gold, and for a gallery not a Pope. Show me one of your new poems, if you've got the guts."

They stared at each other for a descending minute of non-recognition. There was no hatred. They disappeared from each other. "I'll be looking for your work," said Marley.

"Get out of here. Maybe we'll both never make it. Think about that, buddy."

A German Lady Who Got Rich

November, 1982

Edna Muller, slim and passionate, with blue eyes that could go from ice cold to electric flame in a micro-second, smashed herself and her lover in a car wreck in 1968 in Kreuzberg, speeding back to her candled apartment in one of Berlin's great gray working class courtyards built in the Eighteen Seventies. Some fourteen bones broke during the impact. Edna had gotten drunk celebrating her charging with two hundred other intellectuals and artists the barbed wire fence protecting the American Information Center from these weekly charges. Edna was not part of a communist group, although she drank all the free milk she could get at the Free University, handed out along with piles of red-covered books. She got a pure charge out of the charging.

Edna helped form the Berlin underground and read Brecht, Hesse, Bakunin, Kropotkin and Marcuse. She worked at a drug center for heroin addicts that ten of them had put together and gotten funded because West Berlin was to be a showcase for the West. They used theater techniques to get through to the junkies, but every few nights one jumped out of a window. They all lived together in four adjoining apartments and shared their meals.

Edna really wanted to be an actress. Her voice had an extreme range. Everyone told her she had the talent. She had auditioned by request at the Schoenbrunner, but rejected because "your acting is like a public orgasm, everything but acting."

Coming out of the hospital, she encountered a travelling American theater, Shiva's Dance, an amalgam of Living Theater and Dionysius '69. She dropped acid with them one night in the audience participation phase in Media Centrum's hall, stripped off, joined in the singing and strode provocatively through the audience that continued to sit through the remainder of the event.

One of the members of the troupe was a phlegmatic young American with glasses whom she discovered, after she finished fucking him after the second performance and they tripped past silent Turks into a late hours gambling bar, to be a millionaire several times over. Her family had been rich for several generations but had lost it all when the Russians took everything from them, big house and factory, when she was only five. But she never forgot her mother's stories all showing how much better it was to be rich than poor and that being rich depended only on being smart enough, lucky enough and cold-blooded enough.

Edna had never thought of herself as being cold-blooded enough, because she was always "hot". But being with Joe she found rapidly that being hot-blooded sexually did nothing to prevent her being cold-blooded emotionally. She could look at anyone and anything when not on the stage or in bed as coldly as she wished.

He revealed to her on their third big night that he would like to build a small hotel in Katmandu, and call it the Dance of Shiva. He had gotten the idea from the theater directors, Jim and Louise, who spent six months touring Europe and the other six doing yoga and meditation and studying dance in the Subcontinent, preferably Katmandu. This hotel would contain a theater and Shiva Dance could use it the off-season. But they needed a good manager to run it who could move "between worlds", European, American, Asian, and still handle business.

Edna saw her chance and cold-bloodedly said she would go to a famous two-year hotel school in the Alps if Joe would send her

103

so that by the time they built the Dance of Shiva, she would be there to manage it and also start up a local theater.

It turned out that Jim and Louise had become members of the Royal Academy in Nepal for their studies in dance in Nepalese tribal cultures, and so knew members of the Royal Family. Joe, from a Nouveau Riche vulgar family in Florida who had struck it big with a greyhound race track and its associated developments on eight hundred acres they'd been clever enough to buy on mortgage, had been enamored at meeting royalty and discussing an entire nation's problems, history and destiny with people in actual power. This was heady stuff even though his family had sent him to Rutgers to get some intellectual polish. But "polish pewter, it's still pewter," and so Joe fell for the glamour of Nepal, but it was all theater to him. Edna coldly saw that and judged him ripe for the taking. All she would have to do would be split him from Jim and Louise, and she would have a hotel and her own dance company. And, being German, actually Prussian, and not a dumb American hick, she, while licking up some of the glamour, could see only too easily the intrigue, economic, and power struggles going on in this small kingdom directly beset by India and China, pushed by Russia and the United States, torn by the collisions of ancient pasts with glittering and threatening futures.

She understood these naïve Americans only too well. She resolved for the first two years to get their complete trust by being their complete cheerful competent cost conscious, drama loving German stereotype. "Just like Weimar and Hitler and the Kaiser never happened to us," she muttered. "Just give the Americans smiles and efficiency and they think that's all there could be or needs to be in a person."

She did take a local lover at the end of the first year, a trader and a lawyer, who could speak five of the Katmandu languages including Tibetan. Now she had her passport into what really went on around her. She began to swell to Wagnerian proportions and her eyes grew smaller, sharper and firmly encased.

By 1975, she showed Joe how much Jim and Louise cost him. Joe had left the theater and gone back to Florida to live with his ever richer family that moved from being conservative democrats to fanatic republican free market advocates. He had become a hundred millionaire off their latest development into the Everglades. "Just sitting there doing nothing. Once you've seen one alligator hole, you've seen 'em all." "The sixties are over, Edna, it was a gas, but now we've got to look at the facts."

The final blow-up came when Joe refused absolutely to build the new theater next to the hotel. "You can keep doing theater in the hotel and it's a lot less cost that way."

Jim and Louise approached Edna to go ahead on her own and build a dance space. "That was the whole idea, that this would be a creative center, not a cultural museum for visitors from Florida."

Edna told Joe and Joe considered that he'd been betrayed. "They went behind my back!" He gave Jim and Louise ten grand to split Katmandu. "You won't want to stay round here on the street."

"We're the ones who made sure the hotel worked with the people here."

"It's a new day. Now the people here want that tourist money."

Edna laughed. So easy to make Americans fall out with each other. Underneath their perpetual smiles and okays reigned a paranoia deeper than anybody's she knew. Even her fellow Germans. Even the Nepalese. And Americans could not talk anything out. They just "split", or ran away as she saw it from any situation requiring being effort. They operated off feelings and phenomena. Ideas, and therefore long-term objectives were non-existent in their head space. No wonder they revered Jefferson and Lincoln like Gods. They had never thought since. "Of course with

Luther and Bismarck as our Jefferson and Lincoln, we've had to think for ourselves," she said wryly to herself.

She began letting her lover, Ram, buy things using the name of the hotel. This credit allowed them to purchase a new building for his trading goods not far from the Temple of Shiva in Katmandu center. Then she gave him the contract to maintain the hotel, which he used to start their own building company. She invested in property near a five star hotel under construction, whose full plans she knew thanks to disclosures by the hotel inner association. She made sure Joe's family got to meet the King when they came. Joe became the favorite son of the family and was given management of the race track. He sent his Washington friends over to be "shown Nepal", mountains, jungles, tribes, Katmandu, and how to make good buys.

She became quite hefty, even fat, but she carried it well. Ram had an affair or two but so did she. They had a child and got married. She had done it. She had become rich and powerful. She knew in detail what made the world tick in her colorful local culture. She retained access to Berlin and had contacts in Washington.

She had done well in life for a bone-smashed poor girl from Underground Berlin. She was very proud of her Nepalese dance troupe that performed not only for her tourists, but once in Delhi and once in Calcutta.

A Plantation Boss

April, 1984

Brian Nolan taught school in a small village in the Midlands, north of Manchester. His father's company made special parts for the Rolls Royce and Bentleys. He had never had to work for a living. He taught as much to infuriate his father as to feel the power to corner the corruptible minds of most of his class into straight-line thinking as he could, while winking at the rebels with encouraging empathy. Only a few ever escape, he said to himself. D.H. Lawrence was his favorite novelist and Gudrun, the woman in love who got away, his favorite character. Joyce, he thought, was the greater artist and he knew exile, silence and cunning would eventually be his weapons also. He loved Ballard's send up of the hallucinating bourgeois, but he was too subtle to be caught by Marx, much less by the Labour Party though he sometimes voted for it.

He had become a teacher in this remote locality in the Midlands (remoter than the Upper Nile, he called it) because a fantastic pharmaceutical-sex-music scene centered in the area. All those in the know picked up a job on the Railroad, the Schools or the Health System. The weekends were a riot. They had real fun. No holds barred. He thought the Haight-Ashbury could not have gone as far as they were doing. And they were all so cool. Ceremonies at Stonehenge, Avebury, Glastonbury, the Moors, the Downs, Brighton Beach parties, Soho, but mostly in the nearby woods and in the old house on the hill.

Nobody could get in the scene who didn't have and couldn't hold down a job. That was what cooled it, that one rule. No American rebel would ever have thought of that rule. The pharmacy contained only the proven psychedelic drugs plus vitamins, herbs, and homeopathics. Some people used their own occasional prescription amphetamine on occasion but it was looked down or at least sideways on. Heroin was a no-no and cocaine thought to be necessary only to stockbrokers, an occupation none of them would be caught dead in, much less alive in.

And after three years of sex and visions, which he low-keyed as "fun and games", and having saved five thousand pounds, Brian set off for the Amazon with the idea of making a fortune and running a small empire of his own as one of his grandfathers had been reputed to have done in Malaysia. Remnants of that fortune had capitalized his father's life and his own education. Brian's idea was to make a plantation of wood itself, a forest of hardwoods that would turn into millions of pounds and a luxurious life style alternating between a remote area and, say, Rio de Janeiro or Miami.

He worked his way up the great inland sea from Belem to Santarem to Manaus, from Manaus to Leticia, from Leticia to Iquitos. At Iquitos he watched a three hundred foot long section of bank fall into the five knot an hour river carrying five houses down with it. He helped rescue one of the people, who happened to be of an important family, and he became privy to the economic and political secrets of the Upper Amazon. Being a schoolteacher had helped him learn to conceal his ambition, and having watched all the changes in many a scene, he could read people's true sex and power desires explicit as a Hardy novel, especially when their favorite drug, alcohol, relaxed their censor.

He did a favor to the Navy Commandante in regard to livening up the Commandante's dances with the addition of a couple of animated young ladies of sufficiently good background. He got himself into the Ayahuascero scene enough to understand the Indian and Hippie psychologies, exposed as they were to the shaman's full regard for the health of their mind. It was like being allowed to sit in a psychoanalyst's sessions with the rich and noble from Mayfair. Obviously, he would have soon been able to operate very well in London, just as here he now knew Iquitos dynamics.

He bided his time before revealing his goals. Just after his first year in Iquitos, he was approached by two Peruvians who he knew owned a good deal of property in the city, with rumors of much more in Lima and in the jungle. They invited him to spend the weekend with them at their hacienda just outside the city. Brian was introduced to the three lovely visitors from Lima who would join their party. The weekend lasted three full days. Wine and cocaine stoked the studies of maps, the financing strategy, the agreeable interludes with different combinations of the ladies. The whole affair was kept at a certain pace by the older of the two men, both of whom clearly used wine, cocaine, cuisine, and skilled women as a way to efficiently deal with complex affairs and to quickly check out a prospective partner for his ability to concentrate on really important matters while his organism was in an unrepressed state, but at cruising speed, not jostling crudely up and down. Nolan was impressed. So this is what came after the Midlands warm-up. This was his entrance into the big time that he had envisaged, however shadowy it might be.

Basically, Nolan was to be made the general manager of five hundred thousand acres of forest. He would earn $50,000 American a year cash over and above his receipted expenses, his transport, communication, house on the property, apartment in Iquitos, four servants, and two security specialists, personal and property security. He would even earn 1% ownership each year he stayed in, and could walk away with it any time after five years if he wished, otherwise they retained full ownership.

Nolan was to organize a legitimate sawmill and logging operation. If he had these new ideas about recycling, fine. He could replant anywhere he cut as long as he could show he was making a profit of $100,000 a year. He was to be open for inspection by anyone, "even gringos", no matter how or when the government might decide to do it. He was to stay on good terms with the Indians that sometimes used part of that area. They approved of his Ayahuasca training by the shaman. They knew all about it. That's how they knew he wasn't just the usual "blue-eyed shit-head who'd die of terror if not something worse out by himself in the jungle." They also liked that he could enjoy himself with girls without importing a family from Europe or Lima to keep up his morale.

They moved to the billiard table to examine his practical mathematics before detailing his other instructions. Nolan had begun to be quite aware that their estate was highly secure. No one had interrupted them in any way for two days. The girls appeared and disappeared almost on cue. Three quite agile mesomorphs clearly did no servant or maintenance work, yet they hung around the property. The older guy's message penetrated through his brain, suddenly, clearly, with nothing else in it but a few words slowly following each other, falling through that intimate space to impact his organism. Keeping his organism from shivering from these impacts so that his grip on the cue stayed steady took all his attention. The words were registering themselves by their own sheer weight.

"If a small group were to move through your forest, you are not to notice them or think about them. They will not come within a mile of your house, and that close only on rare occasions. It is best if you consider them, and say if asked, that they seem to be some native group with traditional rights of travel. If a small group should set up camp somewhere in your forest, it is much the best, as long as they are there, that you do your logging work in another quadrant of the property. Your two agents would make sure no one from any of these groups is the least trouble to you. Undoubtedly, it is most likely, you will never see or notice them. That is by far the best."

Nolan managed to pull off a three cushion shot.

"I totally agree there should be no hindrance, not even a subliminal one, to any shaman or any traditional person doing anything traditional in your forest," he said.

The older man, Enrique laughed and patted Nolan's back. "We're leaving you here a day with our three beautiful friends and our chef. See us next Friday in my office and we'll complete our understanding. And we will secure all of your residence papers."

Nolan created the life he had dreamed for himself for as long as he could remember. This dream had gotten him through the endless days of teaching the mandated lies to the children, running his little part-time mental concentration camp, gassing to death each heretical mind particle that showed itself, then burning the evidence in pseudo-encouraging remarks to think for themselves. Only the ones he could vibe out, two or three a class, got winked warnings that a duplicitous experiment on their lives was being carried out by uniformed (in sport coats and slacks) guards like himself. This dream had justified him to himself for doing the dirty work.

He invited some of the old gang to visit him, and if they liked it, to stay, enjoy the jungle, and if they needed work, do something useful at the sawmill or counting and measuring trees in some systematic fashion for his data mill. A number of them visited him. He covered all their expenses while there whether they worked or not. Gradually, over two years, a small group of five formed, three girls and an English forester, Edward, and himself. This was a lot better company than the agile but thoughtless Lima girls available.

Nolan began to grow fat from drinking much beer. Wine didn't really taste good to him in hot sunshine or ferocious dampness or on steamy evenings. He asked Enrique and when the supply arrived via one of the agents began to use cocaine daily to watch the house, sawmill, and his group. Two of the girls took up rum. Rum seemed to solve all of their problems. They were happy. And since they were young and smart, they seemed more high than drunk except that they slept later and later and occasionally vomited which was not an aphrodisiac. His forester took up experimenting with many kinds of whiskey, specially imported from the well-known shop on Greek street in London. "I am a scientist," he told Nolan. "I have to test carefully which is best." Nolan further grew to hate Edward because Edward always challenged what he called Nolan's "fatuous optimism". "Actually," he said one night, "you could call it self-serving optimism, your doubling the estimate of trees going to maturity on the property."

"What do you mean optimism, I've carefully plugged in all of the variables given to me by your forestry science itself."

"Yes, but you always take the highest figure in all the variables. That's statistically implausible."

"But not impossible." These daily arguments had taken on a recurrent being of their own. Nolan would reload his beer, Edward his whiskey, and they would continue staring at each other. How had they wound up in this Peter Sellers' caricature of an English club, Nolan would think, and then leave to see Jane or Teresa. Edward would wait for Mary to pull him by the hand to bed.

Nolan was called to Lima every three months. First, by boat to Iquitos and then flown to the capital. "We don't want planes flying in and out of the property," said Enrique. " How are you and your English friends doing on the plantation?"

Fernando laughed. "I didn't know English went in for odd numbers. I always thought they played to get even." Nolan realized Fernando did not understand the English colloquialism and was only trying to be funny about the sex ratio, but remembering that he had learned from his Midland experiments that the subconscious always knew all the meanings of every word even though the conscious mind didn't, he felt a chill go through him. Why would they think they had done something to him for which he would try to "get even". What would they do to him for even subliminally projecting there was anything at all to "get even" about? He became really alert again for the first time in three years. He realized, sickeningly, he had gotten fat, dependent on the cocaine to run the logging, sexually predictable, and that his repression was showing if not yet teeth, at least a grimace. These guys were acute psychologists.

Enrique suddenly said, not unkindly, "Nolan, the jungle's rough, even for the Indians. You want to go to Switzerland to dry out for a month, get back in shape. It's on me. You've done a great job. You want to be in shape to enjoy it."

They took him out to a special nightclub act put on just for them. Strippers gorgeously made up, hair-dried, nailed and perfumed, acting out every projection they could pick up on in the three men's eyes. Nolan felt gasping in his stomach at the brilliant provocations, but knew he was happy in a voyeur's delight for the first time. He could see and feel the art, and not have to deal with the actress.

"Okay," he said, "I'll go to Switzerland."

When he came back, and after the doctor had shown him how his organism was in danger, and he had stayed sober long enough to see his decay, he shipped out the two rumaholics, and brought in an imperious young Lima lady who had become his guru. She only did Tantric sex, no orgasms for the man, and insisted on a herbal vegetarian diet. Nolan secretly masturbated once a week, but otherwise was devoted to his new mistress-guru. "You don't do what I say, I go back to Lima, I make plenty of my own money," she told him. Occasionally, she brought in a young man, another student. She would say. "How can you be jealous of him," she would ask. "Those who know must teach".

"Look," he said one night. "You know what these guys are really doing with this forest, don't you?"

"No, they never told me," she said, "and I never asked. Questions and answers are not the way to truth or professors would be teachers."

"I never asked because they told me not to. Questions and answers would probably be the way to death in my case."

"Why don't you leave?"

"I like the money and power. There's no empire left, so now I've become a mercenary fighting other people's wars, no questions asked. But I don't know from nothing. See not, hear not, speak not, because what can you then speak about if you don't see anything.

He spent a long time that night talking to her, pacing the floor of the great hall. Only later did he remember his voice would echo throughout the big house. He remembered when two days later he found the stabbed body of an Indian in front of the house.

"I think one of these small groups must have killed this guy and dumped him here to get you in bad," said one of the agents. "This Indian probably started thinking too much and then talking to another Indian what his vivid imagination told him." The agent laughed slowly. "Thank goodness you are not an Indian."

"Yeah", said Nolan, "thank goodness."

A week later Nolan headed down to the Amazon and then downstream. He hid at nights. He made sure to go past Leticia in the night and past the first Brazilian outpost. He nearly died a dozen stupid ways, because the river is unforgiving and so is the jungle, and a man in a hurry takes a necessary chance now and then.

He bought his way to Britain after being held up in Manaus by the Brazilian officials questioning him on his entry. The girls of the hotel owner flirted with him in the mornings and evenings. An exile from Brasilia, a dark handsome woman discussed politics with him at a river restaurant and pointed out to him statuesque available girls. "After you talk to me, you could have one of those."

He bought a round trip ticket in London for his Peruvian guru to fly over. She moved in with him but said he could not now be taught anything but diet until he totally "recovered his mind". She found some young Englishmen who needed her instruction and soon had a group around her. Nolan was treated like a sick old man of forty.

"One gangster is enough to serve in a lifetime," he shouted at her. "I'm leaving you before you kill me!" He went back to the Midlands to teach, to read Durrell and Burroughs, to dream again and again of his successful living in an updated Conrad novel.

A Seeker for Reality

March, 1985

Ted Slater loved his Malibu house, its terrace facing straight ahead over the bench into the Pacific. He loved the grunnion run under a full moon, the sight of a gray whale blowing off the coast in their migration, the sharp agility of sea gulls, the splash of the broken waves chilling his face in the winter as he stood on his favorite pile of rocks.

Ted Slater loved his work, discovering "talents". If he discovered three talents a year, he did very well. To discover the talents, he had to work Hollywood, Beverly Hills and Santa Monica which he loved in various ways befitting their differences, these three cities that had represented to him a genuine living Utopia coming as he did from Joplin, Missouri, and a lead mine engineering family and a marketing degree from the University of Missouri.

He had found an older man to be his partner and finance his office, car and open some doors. He had managed to produce a movie for a kick and in a satirical spirit, "The Nail Polisher", that had become a cult movie and made him, over four years playing here and there in the U.S. and Europe, his million that allowed him to buy himself the Malibu house and gave him the prestige of a producer. The contacts from this had also cut him into some real estate deals.

The only thing, he had turned fifty in 1977. Ted had never sniffed a line or puffed the magic dragon. Wine and an occasional cigar is all I need, he would say. He had been married once, and depression and boredom. Neither of them saw any point in continuing to behave like two dogs locked back-to-back.

He had always made fair contracts with his "talents" and pushed their careers. If they weren't crazy about his results as their scope grew, they left on good terms and often recommended new talents to him as "the best guy to start with". He had worked on his image, his walking the talk and talking the walk until he could go anywhere in his three cities. He was a fixture in a changing scene.

That night he went to a party in Benedict Canyon and found himself strangely attracted to the daring eyes of a young Guatemalan. Strolling the superbly landscaped path leading up to a half moon view between two thick trunked eucalyptus sentinels, he caught her willing supple waist. She offered him a toke. He could not break the spell. He did not want to take the slightest risk of breaking the spell. He puffed deeply, alternating with her until they finished the thin delicately rolled object except for a hot roach she flicked into the decomposed granite soil.

The night began to change. Instead of her eyes daring him, he stared daringly into her eyes, deep and deeper, drawn into an endlessly receptive world that nonetheless seemed to be weighing minutely his every advance.

She went back to Malibu with him and they walked the beach for an hour, silently. His senses were sharp, keyed to an apprehension of each perception. The half moon disappeared behind the ocean.

On his bed she sat nude, half-Indian, facing him, sitting cross-legged. He sat before her, this young woman in her twenties, feeling himself a student willing to learn. His "talent discoverer" personality had temporarily left him. He didn't care about coming on to her about her "possibilities". Suddenly, he wished to find out about his possibilities if, the thought flicked through his mind, he still had any other than living out the last twenty years or so of his dwindling life force.

still had any other than living out the last twenty years or so of his dwindling life force.

"You want me to make you real," she said at last. "You want me to open your heart to reality."

He nodded, dumb before her surprising insight that he recognized as true.

"I cannot. My way is not open to you. You are," she paused and then capitalized her words playfully, emphatically, satirically, "a Big Time Operator in Glitter Gulch. But you are a good man behind your woman's hairdo and ultra-violet suntan. Your wish is to become real and if you follow your wish you will find your reality. I will go with you the first step tonight". She extended her legs around him, graceful, and began a long, slow massage with heels, toes, fingers, and hands, interrupting it only with kisses.

Ted never saw her again but learned she was a curendera, expert in herbs, who had a small group of apprentices in the Guatemalan highlands.

Her words reverberated into his daily life. Reality. Certainly his life, successful for twenty years, seemed well functioning, but it did resemble a beautifully lacquered veneer, concealing perhaps some not very remarkable plasterboard with probably some crumbling adobe under it. He wouldn't want to be tested by an earthquake such as disease, old age, death, or some show-all state of consciousness. The whole thing might fall down, crushing him forever in its ruins.

Wandering around in his favorite Santa Monica bookshop, he picked out a book on the subconscious. It had a marker advertising a meeting in it. At the all-day Saturday meeting in the grand garden of a Pasadena mansion, he was given instructions, paper, and crayons. He began to draw mandalas, intricate constructions that seemed eventually to be centered. He stared into them and saw connections in his life he had never seen. How a red-haired girl running at the edge of a grass fire, glancing at him with the night. Yet his drawn construction when he stared into it told him in no uncertain way that these two events were equally real, and that they represented something he called a doorway. Only he had gone into one doorway and not the other, thirty-four years ago when he was sixteen. He realized he had not only not joined the red-haired girl in her run racing the fire, but that he had judged and said to himself, that girl's not for me, I'm not wild enough. He had put himself down, because he knew now that he had never wanted to talk to a girl like that again until he met the Mayan curendera.

And the thing had happened that he had feared would happen with the red-haired girl. The curendera had turned him on, given him a password, and disappeared. He had not been real enough to her to be given more.

Then someone in the group mentioned to him the name of a colleague of the mandala depth psychologist. This man had gone off on a different path to reality from the first. He wished to stare into the body itself to unlock the secrets of its past and potentiality. He used his fingers to stare and probe into every stiffness, every piece of "armor," force every defense to leave and for the emotional truth to emerge and release the body from painful imprints of contacts with the relatively unreal.

Ted had also found that the hashish he had been introduced to, if used as a focusing device, helped him to see deeply into the mandalas he created, so he also used this to relax into the skilled hands of a tall striking blonde who soon had poked, probed, pulled his muscles out of decades-long cramps. By the end of two months of a two-hour session per week, he was raging narcissistically, waving his fists and thrashing on the massage table, trying to battle his father and go his own way. The blonde's strong fingers were Echo to his Narcissus howls, they echoed in his flesh each word that repetitively poured forth until he had exhausted their meaning. Fuck you, fuck you, fuck you went on for half an hour like an automaton controlling his mouth, until at ten minutes he saw he didn't mean it you, fuck you, fuck you went on for half an hour like an automaton controlling his mouth, until at ten minutes he saw he didn't mean it to be a blow against his father but a despair that his mother would fuck his father, howls of incredulity, and the final ten minutes of whispering softly, seductively to all the women he had ever found attractive and turned away from starting with the redhead.

Curiously, as Ted felt his eyes literally grow wider and take in more light from his ever-better seeing of mandala forms concentrating emotion in faces, in traffic jams, in hills, in clouds, in cafes, and as he felt his pelvis separate from his leg and stomach, and his body giving out and taking in more "vibrations", he more and more could see his life as a moving picture, a series of images on a soon burnt-out roll of inflammable celluloid.

If the curendera had opened a door, the place he had entered turned out to be only a courtyard. Now that he was inside the keep, and master of its spaces with mandala and gesture, the castle doors still loomed impregnable.

The blonde superwoman laughed when he told her this, his words spilling out without hesitation or block after her thorough workout. "You're ready to go orgasmic," she said. "In fact, you've really come along. Meet me for dinner."

It had been orgasmic. He found it to be a fantastic tour of the courtyard. He was the local village talent who became a castle dancer. A lot better than working out his image over in the village market place, but he still had no idea of what went on inside the castle where the grand seigneur lived. He couldn't see that being sent back out from the keep as a dancer was much better than being an image polisher down in the guild hiring halls. "After the orgasmic discharge, the charge builds back up again," she said, "and then you discharge completely, it's a cycle." He kissed her hand and disappeared thinking, "I've learned one thing, how to disappear like the curendera. If this were truly real, I couldn't just disappear no matter how clever I was."

quickness of glance and fluidity of movement, these new people would flicker in and out of his vision. Sometimes he couldn't catch one for a month. One day, he watched two of them talk for an hour at a café near the entrance of Rodeo Drive, high ceilinged with wooden tables. When one of them left, the other remained seated and motioned him over with a slight head wave.

He had to speak right out to the man. "I want to reach reality, I've tried for over a year now, I would like to form a search group with some people." "My friend," the man replied, "such groups already exist, you have not seen them because you don't have the key to that door. But you have at least stood on tiptoe and looked through a dark window." The man sat tall, handsome, assured, in sweater, khakis, and thin-soled boots. His voice sounded almost lazy as if assured it would be listened to. The man was clearly not interested in wasting any energy to fascinate.

Ted received an address from the man and went to see a woman who lived high up on Mulholland Drive, her house secluded in a wooded grove. After an evening of review of his life and intentions and an appraisal of his health, she agreed to spend a day with him, twenty-four hours. She warned him to expect nothing, be ready for anything and to keep his aim high.

She administered the dose of two hundred micrograms of lysergic acid diethylamide. The lights and perfume, rugs and pillows were perfectly adjusted to relax Ted's emotions and to assure his intellect that he was in the presence and care of an expert. Not one door opened but many in the next ten hours. Rooms of boredom, of horror, of terror that had him curled up like a fetus, of closing walls and no escape, of talents abandoned, destroyed, shrieking their betrayal, of pressure choking his breath, of contempt. At times she came to him and helped him escape by tagging his hand gently, expertly. It never got better.

When it ended, she gazed at him a long time. "You have had the worst experience I've ever seen. The difference between your image and your reality is the widest conceivable."

"But I've never done anything specially good or bad. I made my way by being correct on details and doing my job."

"You have said your same old story, but what you saw tonight is how you really see your life. This is your door into what you call the great castle. Through the dungeons, torture chambers, sewage pits, and the dead dog heap. You can go back or you can go up. I have brought you to where you at last have a genuine choice." They held each other closely and he loved her like a child who has survived a storm and a nightmare. She gave him a book.

For the next three years Ted studied knowledge. This knowledge made him able to select and attract better talents and get them better contracts, but he cut the business to two talents a year and one real estate deal. He needed lots of time to gain knowledge. The last words she'd said to him propelled his search. "Now you must find a map because, going through the next door, he who has no map may see great marvels but he will surely get lost and getting lost again but deeper is not very good, is it?"

He studied the seven levels of mind in the school of those-accelerating-the-way, the ten techniques of the upholders-of-the-way, the eight branches of the tree of yoga, the eight animals of special paths, the eighteen idiots, the four temperaments, and the infinity of I, as well as the differentiating and integrating possible to attention. He took two months off to wander through Latin America, through back peaks, jungles and broad rivers. In a shady whorehouse in Paraguay at the edge of the Green Hill, staring at the young thin girl, he saw all his knowledge unscrolling before his eyes, registering in his perceptions. "Thank you," he said, kneeling to the girl after he held her hand for an hour. He took his books of knowledge and threw them into the river. Returning to Hollywood, he produced a film on Black Holes and Quantum Discontinuities.

He lost money, but he had learned physics. Masters had opened their doors to the universe to his obedient camera asking for their wisdom.

He did another film on evolution, the power and force and vitality of life in its myriad forms. When he walked in the park toward the old reservoir lake half-forgotten in the heart of Los Angeles, he could see the universe, life, history, sevens, eighteens, fours, sense his body building or discharging sexual energy, glimpse mandala mirrors, one day on hashish, two days on nothing but water and wine, to compare the effects of chemistry.

He went to the cemeteries and the morgue and made a documentary on Death in Los Angeles. Not that different from anywhere else he found out.

Certainly, he had learned to stroll through the great castle, to look through its telescopes, microscopes, talk to its savants, read its books, attend its parties discharging its built-up cosmic energies before explosion, and certainly this way was better than the specializing guild stall or the dungeons below, but reality had to be able to include everything and any specific thing that a man encountered.

He realized one day he'd never find reality because he had fallen in love with seeking it. His seeker left every insight as soon as he found it. Ted laughed and relaxed. He took up a finders keepers losers weepers approach to reality. He realized he had become what he always truly wished to be. He relished nearly every moment.

About the Author

Born in Western Oklahoma and reared in the lingering traditions of the frontier, Dolphin first left home at age 14 to work in California in the War effort. He became a young itinerate fruit picker, lumberjack and machinist, then scholar, intermittently studying the classics and anthropology at Northwestern, Stanford and Oklahoma Universities. He organized for the meat-packers union on the South side of Chicago in the McCarthy period, where he encountered two of his heroes, Paul Robeson and W.E.B. DuBois. After the U.S. Army Corp of Engineers, his formal education continued at Colorado School of Mines, and became a metallurgical engineer specializing in special metals from beryllium to uranium, then Bakers' Scholar at Harvard Business School. He worked on overseas projects with David Lilienthal in Iran and Liberia. One day, Dolphin looked outside of his window on Wall Street, and, spying a Yugoslav freighter heading for Tangier, decided to launch himself on a two and a half year sojourn around the world. On this trip, he had a painting studio in Fez; consulted in a remote medical facility in Vietnam; he met Burrough's and Gysin's Third Mind in Tangier, Nile magicians, Tibetan lamas, Special Forces and Buddhist monks in Vietnam, and many other specialists with rare skills along his path.

Since 1967, Dolphin has continued to travel around the planet, co-founded a theater company, written three books of poetry, three novels, a compilation of short stories, thirty-five plays, and produced and/or directed some eighteen films. He has read at George Whitman's Shakespeare and Co. in Paris, in New York accompanied by Ornette Coleman, at the October Gallery in London with West African musicians, and the Caravan of Dreams in Fort Worth, Texas. His plays have been performed on seven continents, from the ICA in London and Theater du Soleil in Paris, to villages on the Amazon and streets in California, from Wroclaw to Oshogbo. He now performs several times a year with dancers and musicians as Johnny & the Dolphins.